Her Texas Ex

Her Texas Ex

A Dangerous Delaney Romance

Katherine Garbera

TULE
PUBLISHING

Dedication

This book is dedicated to everyone who's ever felt like they didn't belong. I was the "weird" one in my family and spent a big chunk of my time living in what my mom refers to as "Kathy's World", while my family loved and have always supported me in whatever I chose to do, when I left my home and went to school and then out in the world, I've always felt different and not like everyone else. For me reading was the way I found normal. I could sit on the school bus, waiting room or workplace cafeteria with my latest romance novel and my nerves and awkwardness disappeared as I lost myself in the book.

Acknowledgments

Thank you so much to all of the Last Stand authors especially the women who were on our Texas Adventure: Eve Gaddy, Justine Davis, Jane Porter, JoAnn Rock, Sinclair Jayne, Kasey Lane, and Cyndi Parent. It's always so much fun to create something from scratch and with people who I adore!

Chapter One

S OMETIMES, AMELIA CORBYN thought that Last Stand, Texas, was the town that time forgot. Well, except for the busloads of tourists who shopped on Main Street every day, but the rest of the world seemed to have forgotten it, or maybe it was simply that Last Stand had turned its back on the world.

When she'd been in New York, it had been easy to reminisce about her hometown and think of it fondly. The sleepy little town in Hill Country was steeped in history and tradition. But now that she was back, she didn't find the history quite so charming and her own family traditions were bringing to the surface emotions she'd spent years suppressing. It wasn't as if any reasonable person on the planet would have an issue with meeting her sisters at Kolaches, the town bakery, and having the spring special brew that featured orange mocha lattes.

She knew it was unreasonable to sit in her car on one of the hilly streets just off Main, watching the entrance. But she'd been avoiding her mom and she wouldn't put it past her youngest sister Delilah to "surprise" her by bringing their mother. She loved her sisters, but like any close sibling group, there were times when they got on each other's nerves.

Emma arrived first, which made Amelia smile. Of course, her middle sister would be the first—she was always punctual—and from her spot across the street from Kolaches, Amelia noticed Emma picking a table near the window. She tucked a strand of her long reddish-brown hair behind her ear and turned her face toward the sun for a moment before she took a book from her purse and set it on the table.

Emma was the shyest of the three of them and preferred reading to socializing, any day of the week.

The sound of a roaring motor made her turn her head as Delilah rounded the corner on her Yamaha DragStar. It was safe to assume Mom wasn't going to be at breakfast, Amelia thought. Their mother hated the motorcycle that Delilah had brought back from Dallas along with a tattoo on her inner wrist and some baggage that no one had been able to get her to share. All Amelia knew was that Delilah had left a five-star kitchen in the Dallas area and come back here to open the Dragonfly, down by the river. She was a tyrant in the kitchen and out. She was a perfectionist who liked things the way she liked them and didn't hesitate to voice her opinions. Amelia sometimes thought that her youngest sister looked like the sweetest person...until she flashed her temper.

There was a rap on her window, stirring her from her thoughts. It was Delilah, her helmet tucked under her arm and one eyebrow raised.

"Why are you hiding over here?"

"I wasn't. I just got here."

"That would work if I was born yesterday," Delilah said. "But I wasn't. You thought I was going to bring Mom."

"Maybe. I just wasn't taking any chances," Amelia said.

"Mellie, I'm not that sneaky. You know if I was going to bring her, I would have texted you," Delilah said.

"I'm just not ready."

Delilah reached through the open window, put her hand on her sister's shoulder and squeezed. "I know—that's why I came alone."

"What's the deal? I thought we were going to have kolaches and catch up," Emma said. "Why are you two out here?"

"We weren't sure if you were getting to a 'good part' in your book. We didn't want to interrupt," Delilah said, hugging Emma.

Amelia got out of her car and out of habit locked it, but crime wasn't that high in Last Stand.

"I ordered three orange mochas for us and kolaches so let's go," Emma said.

She followed her sisters back into the bakery and waved at Mrs. Parsons and her daughter, Jade, who were both behind the counter. Jade had been in her grade, so they'd been friends when they were younger, before Amelia had dropped out of high school and went off to pursue modeling.

How different would her own life have been if she'd never left?

It was a question she'd spent too much time thinking about over the past twelve years, but she'd never have been able to stay. Even now, she felt anxious at the thought of trying to blend in and be normal. She hadn't been normal since that night…two days before she'd left for New York. Everything had changed, and she'd moved on and never looked back. But now she was here again. Mom was sick and her memories were fading. If Amelia wanted answers, she needed to ask the questions that she'd never had the courage to ask before.

"I'm so happy you're home," Emma said, tucking her book back into her bag. "I do love visiting you in the city, but this is nicer."

"It is," Delilah agreed. "But I'm not holding hands or wearing matching outfits to Minna's birthday shindig."

"Damn, no matching outfits. I was going to put in a call to one of the high-end design houses and see if they could do something haute couture for us," Amelia said, laughing.

"Since our styles are so distinct, I think the time for matching outfits has gone," Emma said. "I'm not wearing that biker chick stuff you like and frankly, Amelia, your clothes scare me."

"How could my clothes scare you?" she asked.

"The price tags. What if I spill something? Or stumble?"

"Then we would get it repaired. And for the record, I think you'd look good as a biker chick," Amelia said.

"Uh, hold on, that's my vibe. Emma's going to have to find her own."

"I'm happy as I am," Emma said. "And with my sisters back by my side. You have no idea what torture it was to go to all the events in town by myself."

"Well, all of the Corbyn girls are back and that's all that matters," Delilah said.

Except she wasn't a Corbyn girl. Not really. And she'd never figured out how to make her peace with that.

THE DELANEY RANCH wasn't exactly close to downtown Last Stand, which was exactly the way his bank-robbing ancestors had wanted it. They'd rob trains, banks and anything else they could get their hands on during the late 1800s, using their ranch as a hideout, and there were days when Cal thought they'd had the right idea by not getting involved in town. But he didn't live in the nineteenth century and making his living as an outlaw had never appealed to him.

He'd been labeled an outlaw on the playing field back in his pro-football days because he'd been the kind of quarter-back who didn't just stay in the box. But a career-ending sack five years ago had put an end to his playing days. The only other thing he'd had going on were some agave vats he'd invested in and the old jailhouse he'd purchased when he'd been feeling nostalgic. Over the years he'd turned that into a successful tequila brand using the old wanted posters of his ancestors as the branding for the liquor. Through his ancestry he was Irish and Mexican, and he had property in Mexico where he grew and harvested the agave that they used for the tequila.

He'd invited his brothers to join him in the business and Braden his youngest brother had taken him up on the offer.

Braden was scary smart when it came to numbers and business, so Cal left the day-to-day running to him. Finn had flat turned him down, preferring to continue his career in the truck league in NASCAR, working his way up over the last few years. He was now a Cup driver, which Outlaw Tequila was a happy sponsor of.

Most days, Cal didn't worry too much about his family or their supposed curse—his dad and granddad had both said the Delaney name wasn't good for a woman, since no Delaney woman had survived past her thirties, including Cal's mom. But he thought that curse was about to be broken. His baby sister Rose was nineteen. She'd made some dumb decisions but hell, what Delaney hadn't? And she was getting her life sorted out. She'd had to—she'd had a baby before she graduated from high school. Cal's nephew was two and a half years old and while he had no use for TJ Maverick, the boy's daddy, Cal loved his nephew. And he was determined to make sure that Delaney Maverick didn't turn out to be the no-good loser that Rose's boyfriend was.

He pulled his Chevy pickup into the spot reserved for him at the storefront of Outlaw Tequila and got out, putting on his black Stetson. Braden's sports car was already in his assigned spot and he noticed there were a few tourists waiting for the shop to open. He glanced back at Main Street. As a teen, he couldn't wait to get out of this place. He'd had a full-ride scholarship to A&M and he'd enjoyed every minute of his time there, playing hard and working hard on the football field and in the classroom. His father, who'd been a heavy drinker and smoker, had gotten ill Cal's senior year and died before Cal had graduated. It had fallen to him to make sure his brothers and little sister were raised. And he'd done the best he could, but he didn't like to think about the ways he'd screwed up.

No matter how much he wanted to blame Rose for falling for TJ's smooth-talking ways, Cal knew if she'd been raised in a better environment…well, maybe things would have been different.

He shook his head. The fight they'd had this morning wasn't the way anyone should start their day. He had told Rose she couldn't marry TJ until she got through college. Heck, she'd just finished high school. She was still a kid. And honestly, he didn't want her to marry the jerk at all. The boy was barely able to hold down a job and he had dropped all of the college courses he'd promised both Cal and his sister he'd take.

"Cal, you got a minute?"

He turned to see Jasper Corbyn walking toward him from the People's Bank of Last Stand on Main Street. The Corbyn family had been bankers in town for generations and back in the day, Cal's ancestors had tried robbing them a time or two. But that was all in the past. And during the annual heritage days when they re-enacted the battle to save Last Stand, Cal and Jasper had some fun impersonating their ancestors.

"Yes, sir," he said. It'd be a relief to have something other than his relationship with his sister to think about. "What's up?"

"I was hoping you could come by the bank sometime

today to discuss the small business loan for the tattoo parlor."

"What are you talking about?"

Jasper tipped his head to the side. "The one you and TJ are opening. I've talked to Dana at Main Street Realty and she says your location is prime. I need to go over a few details with you. I've talked to TJ and he did say he'd be running the daily operation with Rose."

Oh, hell no. "Let me talk to TJ. I didn't think we were at the loan stage yet."

"Fair enough. I think you're smart to do it through the bank instead of privately. When family is involved in money deals, it can cause all kinds of problems. Want me to put it on hold for now?"

This was honestly the first thing TJ had done that made Cal believe the kid was actually thinking of the future. Cal didn't want to stand in his way, but he had to talk to him before he could just sign off on a loan. "Can you give me until after Minna's party?"

"Sure. Take as long as you like," Jasper said.

Jasper left and Cal turned away from Outlaw Tequila, walking instead toward Kolaches. He needed time to think and he'd always done that better when he was outside… Actually he did his best thinking when he was under pressure in the box just after taking the snap on the football field, but he wasn't on the field anymore. This was life, not a game that wouldn't matter in five years. He had to be careful how he played this situation.

HER SISTERS HAD to leave to go to work but since Amelia was only in town temporarily because their mother was unwell and she didn't have anything urgent planned that morning, she stayed behind to enjoy a second latte. Kolaches was busy in the morning with the rush hour crowd stopping by on their way in to the office and as that crowd slowed, the vendors who had downtown businesses started to trickle in. Amelia was just about ready to leave when he walked in.

Cal Delaney.

She'd like to say the years hadn't been kind to him, but they had. When she'd known him in high school, he'd been long and lanky with some overdeveloped arm muscles from working out and playing football year-round. But he'd matured into his frame and now he seemed to be all muscles. He wore a black Stetson, which he doffed when Mrs. Parson greeted him, and his voice was still that deep rumble that made her senses go wild. His jeans fit tight against his butt and thighs and he wore a pair of Kelly Boots on his feet. She sat back in her chair, staring at him, even though she shouldn't.

She'd heard from her dad that he'd been injured during a game and hadn't been able to keep playing football. She also knew he had started a tequila business here in town, and from her friends in New York, she knew his top-shelf Outlaw Tequila was a crowd pleaser.

She didn't stop staring, even when he turned around and noticed her. Lost in her thoughts about him and what a gorgeous man he'd become, it didn't even occur to her to turn away. He moved toward her with the kind of grace and power that male models seldom achieved. He could make a fortune with those cheekbones.

"Like what you see?"

"Um…actually, yes, I do," she said, standing up and holding out her hand to him. "Amelia Corbyn. I'm not sure if you remember me from high school."

"Damn. That's cold," he said, glancing over his shoulder as if to make sure no one was close enough to hear him as he leaned down, resting one hand on the table, and brought his face close to hers. "As if I'd forget the first girl I ever slept with."

She blushed.

"Well, um, yeah, I didn't forget you either," she said. All the sophistication she'd thought she'd cultivated in Manhattan was out the door. He made her feel…just like she'd felt when they'd dated. Those three magical weeks, before her world was shaken and broken and she learned she wasn't really a Corbyn daughter.

"Glad to hear it. I mean I wasn't at my best, but I didn't think it was that horrible. I mean, I wouldn't have run away the next day or anything like that," he said, spinning the chair across from her around and sitting down on it.

She felt the redness in her face and glanced down at the table, turning her latte mug in her hands. "Oh, about that, I'm sorry for the way it might have seemed. There was a lot going on in my life and I had the offer from Elite to go and model for them."

"I remember. Looks like that worked out for you," he said. "Rose is a huge fan of yours. She's always showing me your covers."

"Aw, she was always the sweetest little thing," Amelia said. The Delaney house had been a predominantly male zone when she'd dated Cal. And though his little sister—a card-carrying tomboy—fit in, she'd loved to play with Amelia's makeup when she was over there. "How old is she now?"

"Nineteen. She took a page from your book and dropped out. She has a little boy—Delaney. We call him Lane."

"Wow. It has been a while since I've been back. My sisters didn't mention anything about that. Is she...how is she?" Amelia asked at last. She knew that despite it being the twenty-first century, small towns weren't always accepting of teenage moms.

"She's good. We have help with Delaney and Rose is still living at home. She's been going to college over in Austin," he said.

To anyone else, it would seem as if she was catching up with an old friend, but there was more to it than that. Maybe it was because of the way she'd had to leave, but he'd always been someone she'd never been able to forget. She thought about that night a lot. She had no regrets about sleeping with him. She'd known once she got to New York her life would be different and she had wanted her first time to be with...well, someone she'd cared about.

"Enough talking about my family," he said. "What are you up to these days?"

"My folks asked me to come back for a while. I've temporarily opened an agency here in town to scout for talent and to teach kids what they need to know if they want to model. I'm doing some classes on manners on the side because the Texas Women's League asked me to."

"Sounds…"

"Boring? Silly?"

"Neither of those. Sounds perfect for you. And if playing pro ball taught me anything, it's that the world outside of Last Stand takes some adjusting to," he said, at last.

"It sure does. Took me a while," she admitted.

"Me too," he said. His phone pinged, and he glanced down at the screen. "See ya around, Amelia."

He walked out of the door and she watched him leave. She hadn't anticipated seeing him or talking to him, having been so focused on her issues with her mom, but she was suddenly glad to be back.

Chapter Two

AMELIA HAD ALWAYS tried to miss Minna Herdmann's annual birthday extravaganza. The one-hundred-and-two-year-old kept proving the doctors and her critics wrong by celebrating another year when some, okay most, residents expected her to have kicked it before this. Amelia didn't mind celebrating Minna and actually enjoyed the fact that the centurion was still here to celebrate.

But the real reason Amelia didn't like coming was that Minna unfailingly tried to corner her to give out her unsolicited advice. And it was advice that Amelia knew she should probably take. Let go of the past. She knew what Minna would say because Amelia's memaw—Priscilla, a spry seventy-two-year-old—had been giving her the same advice for years.

And anyone else would have let it go...or would they have?

"Why are you staring at Minna?" Delilah her youngest sister came up next to her and handed her a margarita. Delilah had long blond hair that she habitually wore in a braid when she was working in the kitchen at her farm-to-table restaurant—the Dragonfly.

"Just trying to figure out how I can wish her a happy birthday and congratulate her on her long life without being alone with her. You saw what she did to Lily Jones—telling everyone to back off so she could have a word."

Delilah laughed. "There's no way you are going to get out of it. If she wants a word with you, she'll get it."

"I know. That's why I was staring," Amelia said, taking a sip of her margarita. She could tell it was made with the local Outlaw Tequila. It was a good quality tequila sourced from agave in Mexico and made locally outside of town on part of the Delaney ranch property.

She had to give Cal props for turning his family's notorious past into a win and making his Outlaw Tequila one of the top brands in the world. There was so much—

"Don't stare at Cal," Delilah said elbowing her. "If you don't start acting like you're at a party, I'm going to tell Memaw you're confused about which one of her beloved stuffed dogs you get when she dies. Then you'll have something to distract you."

"Don't you dare," Amelia said. "I don't know what my deal is today. I'm just feeling so out of sync with everything lately."

"You're just not used to being back yet. When I came home from Dallas five years ago, it was nine months before I could adjust to the small-town vibe. I mean, of course, we grew up here, so it shouldn't be a shock, but it sort of is," Delilah said.

"You're right."

"I know I am. I'm smart...not Emma smart, but I do

okay."

"You're plenty smart," Emma said, coming up to them. "I just read more."

"Reading is the key to life," Amelia said. Their mom had raised them with books piled in every room. Because of the secret her mom had kept from her for so long, she had never been able to enjoy coming back. She'd even avoided Memaw because she knew that her outspoken grandmother would tell her to get to the heart of things with her mother. But she couldn't. She didn't want to dig into that painful time in her life. She had found a way to cope and it mainly meant staying away from Last Stand.

Or it had…until her mom got sick.

That's when her dad had asked her to come home. He'd said this might be the last chance for them.

"Or a great escape from it," Emma said. She wore her hair in a low bun at the back of her neck and several rusty-brown tendrils had escaped to frame her heart-shaped face.

Amelia always thought that Emma was the most beautiful of the three of them. And she had a serenity about her that Amelia also envied. "Why are you two huddled over here? Grandmother will only be distracted by Jacob Haines for so long and then she will notice us. And that never leads to anything good."

"Agreed. We should all split up and mingle, but Amelia was staring at Cal," Delilah said.

"You were? Are you interested in him? He's on the heritage committee and they are meeting at the library on Wednesday evening. I could arrange—"

"No. No, don't arrange anything. I'm just a mess today. My studio is apparently in a flood zone, Mother asked me to meet with her alone and I didn't respond so Daddy texted me about it, so you know I'm in trouble," Amelia said.

"Why didn't you respond?" Emma said. "Mother wouldn't have asked if it wasn't important, and you know she's sick and doesn't want to push you. But I think she wants to get everything in order."

Amelia's heart broke when she heard that. Her feelings for her mom were complicated but she loved her. She was mad at her and had been since she'd left Last Stand, but she didn't want her to die. She wished there was some bit of magic that would make her understand what had happened. "I know. Because I'm a horrible daughter who can't let go of my issues," Amelia said.

Delilah put her arm around her sister's shoulders and Emma did the same. "You have to talk to her soon."

"I know."

It didn't need saying out loud, but their mother was sick, which was why Amelia had finally come home. She knew she had to make peace with her mom, but knowing it and doing it were two very different things.

"Hello, ladies," Cal Delaney said coming over to them with full margarita glasses.

Again, she was struck by his good looks. The ten years since she'd last seen him had only served to enhance his sexiness. As a boy his face had been all angles but time had changed that into a strong jaw, firm lips and high cheekbones. His years of playing professional football had ensured that his body was muscular and lean. She knew she was staring at him again but it was hard not to.

She hadn't looked her fill the other morning it seemed. Plus there was something just so rugged and damned sexy about the way he carried himself. It was hard to look away.

"Cal," Delilah said. "Thanks for the refill. I'm going to go mingle. Don't let my sisters turn into wallflowers."

"Yes, ma'am," Cal responded to Delilah as she took her drink and walked away, dropping her empty margarita glass on the tray of a passing waiter.

"I see Landry from the Friends of the Library. I need to speak with her before she disappears," Emma said, leaving. "See you next week, Cal."

"Looking forward to it, Emma," Cal said.

Amelia looked down at her margarita glass. Honestly, there wasn't enough tequila in the world to make her stop feeling awkward today.

"And then there were two," he said, his voice just as deep as it had always been, but low-pitched so that it traveled no further than her ears.

"Yes. I meant to say…I suppose you wondered why I left right after the night we spent together." She hadn't fully explained the situation the last time she'd seen him. And she hadn't been able to stop thinking about him.

"One would say that," Cal said.

CAL HADN'T EXPECTED to see Amelia today. He'd become

pretty good at the jovial smile and faking it as an upstanding citizen of Last Stand. He had outlaw roots and he was always more comfortable in jeans and T-shirt than a suit, but Minna's birthday party required him to play the part. After all the changes in his life, he was so used to rebuilding that when things seemed to be going well, it made him edgy.

Like right now—his brothers were all doing well in their careers and he had convinced his baby sister Rose to go back to school and hold off on marrying her loser baby daddy. So Cal had thought everything was right in his world and then Amelia had walked into the party looking more beautiful than a woman had the right to. He was struck dumb, just like he'd been in high school. He'd looked around for someone to distract him but his brother's friend Red Aldean was busy teaching a group of kids the right lure to use to catch perch in Hickory Creek, a spur off the Pedernales River. And his brother was flirting with some girl that Cal didn't know so he'd been left to his own devices—standing there staring at temptation and hating that Amelia still had any power over him.

She'd been his first. He'd always attributed that fact to the reason why he couldn't forget her. She'd also left him…well the entire town, hell, the great state of Texas the day after they'd had sex. It had made the man-boy he'd been start asking some questions he still couldn't answer.

And now she was back. He'd seen her one other time in the years since she'd left Last Stand. They'd been at an NFL/United Way gala in New York and she'd been someone else's date. He'd still been with his former fiancée Sheena then, so it had seemed fitting to him.

Today, she wore her ebony hair in a blunt bob that accentuated her cheekbones and drew his eyes to her lips. Her mouth was full, and he wondered if he'd just fantasized how soft her lips were and how right they'd felt under his. It had been a long time since he'd held her, but he remembered how she'd fit so perfectly in his arms. Of course, he'd filled out since high school, so they might not be that good together now.

Yeah, right.

"I'm sorry I didn't say anything before I left," she said. "You were probably not even bothered, but leaving you like that has stuck with me for a long time."

He was surprised she had brought that up, but it had been on his mind too, ever since he'd heard she'd come back. He'd never understood why she'd left. "It bothered me. I showed up at your house the next morning to pick you up and Jasper told me you were gone," he said. Mr. Corbyn had been intimidating back when Cal had been in high school but the two of them had become friends once he'd become an adult.

"Yeah, that was a really horrible thing for me to do," she said. "It had nothing to do with you."

"Wow, really?" he asked. "If it had nothing to do with me then why'd you sleep with me before leaving?"

"Damn, why don't you go straight to it?" she asked. "I suppose I wanted a good memory to take with me."

He didn't know how to respond to that. "I guess that means I didn't make you run away."

"Did my dad say I ran away?" she asked. "My parents weren't too happy about me leaving, but they knew I was going to New York."

"Yeah, that's what he said," Cal responded. He now knew precisely nothing more than he had before he'd started this conversation, but he felt like he could let go of the feeling that he'd been a contributing factor to her leaving. "We never have to talk about that night again, if you don't want to."

"Great," she said, offering him a small smile. "I've felt like a d-bag over my behavior for a long time."

He shook his head, wishing he'd brought a bottle of tequila with him, so he could knock back a couple of shots, but just smiled instead. "Don't. It's all in the past."

"I love that you made the old jail into a storefront. Some of your Delaney outlaw ancestors must be crowing over that," she said.

He let her change the subject and then after catching her up on the tequila business, he said goodbye and walked away from her. He'd thought it would bring him closure, that the answers she'd given him would be enough to let him have a win in walking away, but it wasn't. He still wanted something more from her, but he had no idea what.

And with the Delaney curse, it wasn't like he expected a different outcome. No Delaney woman had ever lasted. They were a lawless clan, except for Rose. She was the only Delaney woman standing and Cal intended to do everything in his power to ensure that his baby sister stayed that way. And if that meant going behind her back and making sure her boyfriend was man enough for her, then so be it.

THE CARRIAGE HOUSE restaurant had been here before Last
Stand had officially been a town. In the mid-1800s, it had
been a carriage house for travelers heading north toward Fort
Worth or back east, but in the last decade it had become the
number one party venue in town. The place was decorated
for Minna's birthday with flowers, balloons and other festive
Texas-themed décor that represented the decades that Minna
had been alive. Chairs and tables made judicious use of the
space, maximizing seating for all the of town's inhabitants
who would be in attendance today.

Minna caught her eye and waved at Amelia in that regal
way she had, and Amelia toyed with the idea of pretending
not to see her. But she knew she'd catch hell from her
grandmother if she did that.

So she made her way around to Minna to give her a
birthday greeting. The older lady was holding court in the
center of the room, as well she should. Her silver-gray hair
had been plaited into a crown braid and her eyes sparkled
with delight. Amelia was pretty darn sure that Minna liked
being the center of attention and that was one thing Amelia
could understand. It was easier to get out of her own head
when other people were watching her.

"Happy birthday, Minna," Amelia said, dropping a kiss
on the older woman's cheek. She was thin and wiry-looking,
wearing a pale blue gown that made her eyes seem brighter

than they normally were.

"Thank you, my girl. It's good to see you back in town," Minna said.

Amelia nodded. "I guess so." Even though she'd been back for ten days, it had been a busy time and Amelia hadn't ventured into town for any social events apart from coffee with her sisters. Other than that she'd pretty much limited herself to grocery shopping in Austin, a good two hours' drive from Last Stand, and attending church because her parents expected her to. And that was it. She'd been focused on working on the house she'd rented and avoiding her parents. She'd only come back because of her mom's health issues—not to talk about the past...no matter how much the past dominated her every waking moment.

"I know you don't want my advice and to be fair, your grandmother told me it was none of my business. But I am over a hundred, so I figure Priscilla really needs to remember to respect her elders."

"I'll remind her of that," Amelia said unable to stop the grin on her face.

"You do that. While you're at it, I think you need to set-tle with the past. You may have left Last Stand to see the world, but you've come back here the exact same confused girl who left."

Amelia wished she could ignore Minna's words, but she knew they were the truth. "Some things are easier said than done."

"The hard bits are always like that. But you just have to get some gumption and do it," Minna said.

"Minna, you make me feel like a coward," Amelia admitted. "I've been trying to get my head around things and I can't."

"You're trying too hard," she said. "If I've learned anything living all these years, it's that there are some things that don't make sense if you overthink them."

Maybe Minna had a point. She glanced up, hearing her mom's laughter. Her mother had her head thrown back and held on to her dad's arm as she laughed. And as much as she had unsettled issues with her mom keeping the fact that she wasn't Jasper Corbyn's biological daughter a secret from her, that laugher brought a smile to her face and Minna reached over, squeezing her hand.

"Now go and get me one of those margaritas that Cal is peddling. I haven't had one in years."

"He makes them strong," Amelia warned her.

"Just the way I like them," Minna said with a wink.

She left Minna's side and asked the waiter to bring her a margarita, then she went over to talk to her mom. Her dad shouldn't have had to text her to make her respond to her mother, but things were always more complicated than Amelia wanted them to be. She always thought she'd made her peace with the past until she saw her mom and it all came rushing back.

She got close to her parents. Both in their fifties, they looked younger. Her mom wore her auburn hair in a short pixie cut that had some length to it, spiked up around her head. She had her gold-rimmed glasses on and wore a turquoise dress that brought out the green in her eyes.

Looking at her mom, Amelia could hardly believe she was so unwell, but she knew how concerned her dad was. Her dad had on a pair of dress jeans and boots, a button-down shirt and a sports coat. His hair was still blond, though streaked with gray now, and he was clean-shaven.

In her heart, she felt that pain that always hit her when she saw them. It started out with love and ended in betrayal and she knew she had to let it go. She'd been sixteen when she'd found out the truth and it had changed nothing but her reality. Her sisters and her parents were the only ones who knew the secret, but they'd never discussed it.

Red Aldean walked up to her. "I heard you were back in town. My cousin is thinking about signing her daughter up to take lessons at your studio. She wants to be a model," he said.

"I'm glad to hear that."

"It's great to see all the Corbyn girls back together again," Red added. He'd been at school with her and for as long as Amelia could remember, he'd been happier outdoors than inside.

She nodded and turned away from her parents. This was why she'd stayed away. She wasn't a Corbyn girl. Not really. Biologically, she had a different father, but no one knew that outside of those involved in the whole sordid thing. When she'd learned the truth at sixteen, it had rocked her world and for the life of her, Amelia had never figured out how to right it again.

Chapter Three

"I GOT YOUR text about a business loan for TJ," Braden said coming over to him. His brother might be the youngest of the three of them, but he had always been the most serious. He was a lot like Cal remembered his mom being. She'd been the one to hold things together and Braden did the same now.

"What do you think?" Cal asked, glad to be discussing something he actually understood rather than thinking about Amelia. Two conversations in as many days and he couldn't get her out of his mind. He wanted to believe it was simply the way she'd left when they had been teenagers. They'd never had any closure. Closure was a big deal, right? According to all of his exes, he sucked at it.

"I think…I'm not sure, honestly. I can see where this might be a good idea because he needs focus and Rose is determined to have him as her man, but on the other hand, he does tend to run through money really quickly."

"Yeah, I'm on the same page," Cal admitted. "I'm glad Jasper stopped and mentioned it because it gives us some time to discuss it. But TJ should have come to us first."

"You punched him the last time he was at the ranch,"

Braden reminded him.

"You're point being?" Cal asked. He knew he had a short temper where TJ was concerned. Part of it was just the way the kid was. He wouldn't look Cal in the eye, he mumbled when he spoke to him and he'd knocked Cal's sister up... That was hard to forgive. He'd never even acted like he needed to get his shit together. So instead, Rose was working two jobs, taking care of her baby and going to college. Cal wanted a better man for Rose.

But as Braden had said, Rose wanted TJ.

"What a damn mess," Cal said.

"Yeah. Let me run the numbers and see if we can find someone to run the shop for him. Supposedly, he's good with a tattoo needle."

"Actually, I know a guy in Houston... We might be able to convince him to come up here," Cal said, thinking of the guy who did a lot of the team's ink when he'd been playing pro ball.

"Perfect, let me know what you find out," Braden said, tossing back the last swallow of his tequila. "We also need to discuss the Bluebonnet Festival. I was thinking we could use the branding and booth setup we used at Texas Motor Speedway last November. The Outlaw poster photo booth was pretty successful on the day and on social media. Rina is running the numbers—"

"Dude, we're at a party. Stop working for like twenty minutes," Cal said as he clapped his hand on his brother's shoulder. If there was ever a guy who needed to get laid, it was his workaholic brother.

"You mentioned the loan," he said as if that meant they should talk shop.

"Fair enough. I just want you to relax sometimes," Cal said. "Just thinking about your workload stresses me out."

"Unca!"

Cal turned to see his nephew Delaney toddling toward them. He wore a pair of jeans, hand-tooled custom-made Kelly Boots with the Delaney crest and a PAW Patrol T-shirt. He had a tiny black Stetson perched on his head. Cal stooped down with his arms outstretched as his nephew ran to them. He scooped him up and stood looking for Mrs. Hanson who had been watching Lane until the party.

"Sorry, Cal. I swear I didn't even look away. He squirmed to get down and then took off," Mrs. Hanson said. "He's got Rose's mischievousness."

"He definitely does," Cal said. Lane put his arm around Cal's neck and held him loosely. He'd been torn when Rose had first told them she was pregnant. He'd just suffered his injury and he'd been trying to figure out what to do next. Coming home...well that seemed like a dead end. Not because of the place, but because of what it represented. Braden had been running Outlaw Tequila and honestly didn't need Cal around.

He'd never felt more useless until Delaney had been born. And he'd realized how young nineteen was when he looked at Rose. At nineteen, Cal thought he'd known it all, thought he'd been mature. In hindsight, he'd had a hell of a lot of growing to do.

"Where Mama?" Delaney asked.

"At school," Cal said. "She'll be here soon."

"You think so?" Braden asked. "She texted me to say you were being an overbearing jerk."

"Yeah, well, she and I don't agree on everything," Cal said, handing Lane to Braden who tossed him up in the air and caught him before turning toward the snack table to get their nephew something to eat.

"She wants to marry TJ," Cal said to Braden when Mrs. Hanson was out of earshot.

"The hell she does. I thought we decided she'd finish college first," Braden said.

"Yeah, we did. She's ticked at me, now, but TJ might be getting his act together," Cal said. He didn't want to get too excited about TJ's prospects because the kid had bailed before. He'd freaked once Rose had given birth and ran off for three months. Cal admitted that he'd never forgiven TJ for that. The kid had come back though and seemed to be trying.

"God, I hope he sticks with the tattoo thing," Braden said. "I don't know what Rose will do if he ghosts again."

"Oh, if he ghosts her again, I'm going to make sure he stays gone," Cal said, every bit of his outlaw Delaney blood and big brother instincts coming to the fore.

"You need to make sure he knows that," Braden said.

"I think that's why he put me down as the cosigner on the loan. He's gutsy. Almost makes me like him."

AMELIA'S GRANDMOTHER LAUGHED in that way some women did, loud and full of joy, making anyone who heard it smile. Amelia noticed Mr. Timmons smiled every time her grandmother laughed but he didn't approach the group where Priscilla held court with a group from the local animal shelter, including Lea Dunwoody, who had been a few years behind Amelia in school. Amelia really needed to get out a bit more. Every memory she had with the people in Last Stand was tied to school and they'd all been out for a while.

Her grandmother noticed her watching and waved her over. Memaw Corbyn had made a point to visit her four times a year while she was in New York. The first time she'd shown up, Amelia had only been there for a month and was a little...short with her. But Memaw had just told her to settle down; she was still her grandmother and always would be.

Memaw had also told her there was more to the story that had sent her running to NY, but Amelia had been too young and too stubborn to listen to her. So instead, they both agreed to let it lie.

She and Priscilla had always been close. In fact, Memaw doted on her and her sisters like they were special angels— her words. When she'd learned that Jax Williams, the legendary country music singer, was her biological father she'd run to her grandmother's house. And her grandmother had listened and just loved her. She didn't try to explain or justify the lies that Amelia had been told. Memaw had just hugged her and said that life sucked sometimes.

She joined her grandmother and her memaw took her

hand and squeezed it. "I was just telling Lea about Christy and how she's getting on in age."

She arched one eyebrow at Lea who just smiled. She wasn't sure how many people in town had realized that her grandmother had owned a dog named Christy for the last…well for at least thirty years. She just kept naming them all Christy. She loved that name and thought it was perfect for a dog.

"I have some new senior dog treats in my bakery. Priscilla wasn't sure if they would be okay for Christy, so I was telling her about the ingredients."

"I don't know much about your business, Lea. I mean Delilah mentioned it was a dog bakery…"

"Yes. It's called Good Boy! When Mom and Dad retired to Florida, I took over their storefront on Main Street—only I'm not really good enough to compete with Kolaches or the pie shop. But I am good with pet treats, so I figured I'd give it a try. It's been going well so far."

"I love that. I'm in the market for a pet," Amelia said. "Someone to keep me company." Even though she didn't plan on staying in Last Stand for long, she thought it would be nice to have a pet while she was there. And she could give it to one of her sisters when she left.

Lea laughed and nodded at her. "Man's best friend has always been better company than man."

"Depends on the man," Priscilla said. "But I have to agree. Christy is sweet company and doesn't make comments about my obsession with old Sean Connery movies."

"We all need more of that in our lives," Lea said. "I'll

have a booth at the Bluebonnet Festival next weekend, next to the pet rescue, so be sure to stop by. Maybe you'll find someone to take home with you."

"I will," Amelia said.

"What are you two up to?" her mother asked, coming over to them. Her mom looped her arm through Amelia's. She knew better than to pull away, and besides, she liked this.

She heard her grandmother answer, but she was busy trying to make sense of the chaos inside of her. She loved her mom more than she'd be able to say and there were times when she'd reached out to her in New York, when she'd needed her mom, and she'd always come, no questions asked. They hadn't talked about Jax or any of that, but her mom had supported her in whatever she needed, and then Lilly Corbyn had gone back to Last Stand.

Damn.

Why couldn't she just let it go?

She'd always wanted to go to New York and have a fabulous life away from this small town. In one moment—and with one secret—she had gotten everything she wanted, everything that her sixteen-year-old heart could have wanted. But the price had been too high. She'd never wanted to give up being a Corbyn to get it.

"Right, Amelia?" her mom said, turning to look at her.

"I wasn't listening."

"That's all right," her mom said. "Lea was mentioning that the downtown tourist season seems to be expanding. We'd noticed the same thing at my shop."

Her mom had a memorabilia shop on Main called Texas Memories. Her parents had been encouraging her to work there until her modeling agency got off the ground, but she'd resisted and come up with every excuse not to do it. But her mom's health issues made it hard for her to keep the store open, and her two assistants had lives outside work too. The doctors were still puzzled by Lilly's symptoms. She was having occasional memory loss issues and problems with the strength in her legs. But still, she had refused to use a cane to walk.

"I'm going to start helping Mom out and work some of her shifts," Amelia said.

Her mom tipped her head back and looked over at her, surprise clear in those crystal blue-green eyes of hers as she blinked. She could see how much that meant and Amelia felt mean and petty that she'd held out so long, but her mom just leaned her forehead against Amelia's arm as if there was nothing to forgive.

"You Corbyns always stick together, don't you?"

"We do," her grandmother said. "Lea, would you like to come to Sunday dinner next week? With your folks living in Florida I know you must miss them."

"Thanks, Mrs. Corbyn, I'd like that," Lea said.

Before they could make any further plans, there was the sound of screeching tires, and then the sickening sound of a crash. Everyone scrambled at the party. The doctors, police and emergency first responders all took off running toward the sound. Amelia wasn't sure what to do but her mom started following the crowd to see if she could help.

THE SCREAM OF tires and then a loud crash broke the party atmosphere and Cal saw Police Chief Highwater and Doctor Graham McBride go running, along with a few other guests. He followed suit. While he had no official medical training, he'd been in enough fights over the course of his life to have more than a working knowledge of general first aid. He stepped off the patio and onto Main Street, noticing the tourist bus that had crashed into Verflucht, the wine-tasting room that August Wolf hadn't had a chance to get opened yet.

He ran toward the van looking for what had caused the crash and as his gaze moved to the other vehicle, his heart started racing, and he heard a scream ripped from somewhere deep inside of him.

Rose's truck.

Oh, dear God. He had tunnel vision as he ran toward her. He had to get to his baby sister.

He was running before he was aware of what he was doing. He got to the flaming upside-down vehicle as Shane Highwater pulled a body from the back seat. He spared a glance for Jake, the kid who worked on the ranch with Rose and took classes at the college over in Austin with her. He moved closer to the truck, trying to get to his sister. But Highwater held him back.

"Don't. The driver and the other passenger are deceased," Shane said. "There's nothing for you to do."

His heart felt like it was being ripped from his chest. He

was breathing as if he'd run a marathon, and his mind really didn't want to believe what his eyes were showing him. "It's my sister," Cal said. "I can't—"

"The fire department will put the flames out," Shane said, drawing him back. "Then we will get her out."

Get her out? What did that even mean? Rose was lost and he threw his head back and screamed with the pain of not being able to protect her.

CAL PUNCHED AT Shane until he was free, stepping away from the police officer as his brothers ran over to the burning truck. Braden looked like he was going to hurl, tears silently streaming down his face while holding Lane in his arms.

His nephew started crying as he looked at his mama's truck. Cal went over to his brother and nephew and pulled them into his arms. They were all shaking and crying. He was the eldest. This fell on him. He was the head of the family and needed to make this right. But Cal was at a loss. At a total loss. Nothing in his life had prepared him for this moment. He felt a hand on the small of his back. Amelia stood there, shock on her face, and he couldn't speak to her.

"Cal, are you going to be okay?" Amelia said, stepping closer to him. Her face was pale as she reached out a shaking arm to him.

"That's my sister's truck," he said, the words guttural, torn from somewhere deep inside of him.

She put her arms around him and held him. He hugged

her back, buried his face in the crook of her neck, the strawberry scent of her hair almost hiding the acrid smell of the burning truck.

She rubbed her hands up and down his back, giving him comfort.

He stepped back, wiping his eyes with his fingers, trying not to look at the truck.

"Oh, Cal. What can I do?" she asked.

He shook his head. Make this all go away? But he was a realist and knew that wasn't possible.

"Let me take care of Lane," she said, moving over to Braden and taking the little boy. Amelia tucked him closer to her chest and rubbed his back. "You want to come with me?" she asked the little boy.

He was aware of Jasper moving around behind him and Delilah and Emma were there as well. The Corbyns had come to help them. He was grateful but he couldn't even talk. Jasper just squeezed his shoulder.

"You do what you need to for Rose. We've got Lane," Jasper said.

"Thank you," he said.

Behind the older man, he saw the tour bus that had crashed into the wine shop and the organized chaos as all the emergency personnel took care of the injured. He should help, but he was stuck there. Staring at the vehicle that he'd bought for his sister. Thinking about the last time he'd seen her and how he'd yelled out the door after her to get her shit together.

Damn.

What the hell was wrong with him?

Hadn't he learned anything growing up with a bitter, angry man?

He was becoming his father and there was no way that was a compliment.

"Cal?"

With each inhalation, the smell of the burning truck filled him, and he stood there, helplessly, watching the flames. The fire department arrived, but honestly it was as if he was viewing everything from a great distance.

Amelia, Lane in her arms, came over and hugged him again. The child looked up at him and he felt like crying again. He knew nothing about raising a kid. What if he screwed up with Lane the way he had with Rose?

"Don't worry," Amelia said, touching his jaw. "I'm here and I'll help you. I'm going to take Lane back to the Carriage House, and then to our house after. You do what you need to do," Amelia said. She hugged him and then she walked away with his nephew, but he was barely aware of it.

Braden came over to stand next to him. Shoulder to shoulder, they watched over Rose as her body was removed from the wreckage. He was aware of ambulances coming and going, taking the injured away, but it was as if it was happening to someone else.

"There were two deceased in the truck," Shane said coming over. "One male severely injured."

"Do you know who the other person in the truck is?" he asked.

"We can't identify him yet. We'd be waiting on the girl

if you hadn't identified your sister," Shane said.

"Damn. The boys in the truck with her were probably TJ Maverick and Jake Fry."

"Thanks for that. Y'all go now. I'll come find you when this is over," Shane said.

Cal shook his head. "We'll stay here until it's done."

Shane just nodded and then walked away, and Cal turned to his brothers.

"I pissed her off this morning, telling her how to live her life. She shouldn't have been driving."

"Stop it," Braden said. "Don't do that. Rose is gone, and it's likely TJ is too. We need to get our shit together for Lane. He's going to need us more than ever. We can't let the guilt consume us. Remember how Dad was?"

Braden was right. "Damn, Bray, I thought we'd seen the last of that damned curse."

"Me too," Braden said. Cal noticed his brother was blinking and just drew him into his arms. They put their heads together as they clung to each other and tears flowed. They would have each other's backs. He wasn't about to let this turn any of them into the bitter man their father had been.

He cried for Rose's life, cut short, and for his own weaknesses. He'd failed her. But he promised himself he wouldn't fail her son.

"What are we going to do?" Braden asked.

"Raise Lane to be the best man he can be, and never let Rose's spirit die," Cal said.

Chapter Four

AMELIA SAT IN the Carriage House playing with the toddler who wasn't exactly sure what he'd seen. Oh, God. This cute little kid was going to have something to deal with when he was older. She heard from her dad that Lane's father had been in the vehicle as well. She knew it would be better if he didn't remember this day and hoped she was distracting him enough.

But she knew from her own experience that some moments in life never seemed to fade. She looked down at Lane and promised herself she'd do her part to make sure he had enough people who loved him in his life that he wouldn't dwell on the loss.

She wasn't at all able to process that sweet Rose Delaney had died. How was this little boy going to manage? Amelia wiped away a tear as she noticed Lane looking up at her.

The Carriage House was bustling with activity as first responders had set up base operation. If there was one thing she loved about Last Stand, it was the community. Yes, those same people would nip in everyone's business and gossip all day long, but they also always had each other's backs. She found a quiet area and sat down with Lane, making sure he was occupied with a pad of paper and a pen from her purse.

Her friend Lea came over to check on them and the look on her face mirrored what Amelia was feeling when she glanced over at Lane.

"Do they know what happened? Who was driving the truck?" Lea asked.

"I'm not entirely sure, but I think it was Rose Delaney," Amelia said.

"Oh my God," Lea said. She reached over and fixed Lane's hat on his head, then gave Amelia a look that she interpreted to mean 'that sucks.'

"I am keeping this one occupied until things settle down," Amelia said.

"Good idea. I'm going to see if they need any more help," Lea said, as she turned and walked back toward Main Street.

Her sisters were both working alongside their father who had been a community leader for as long as Amelia could remember. She felt that pang she always did when she confronted the truth about her parentage. Yet at the same time, she felt pride and admiration for her family.

Priscilla was with her group of cronies, including Clara Perkins the town's unofficial matchmaker. Amelia overheard them talking about rides for those who weren't hurt and then food for those who were. The Texas Heritage Women's group—which the older women belonged to—had been in Last Stand since the beginning. They were always among the first to offer to help out in a crisis.

She could hear the sirens and the acrid scent of smoke

filled the air. The Carriage House had been abandoned midparty so there were half-filled plates and glasses holding drinks that had become watered down from melted ice. Amelia knew that she needed to keep Lane distracted, far away from the accident. But she really didn't know much about children. She'd hugged the little boy, but he'd squirmed to be put down. He looked scared and she had no idea how to comfort him.

She stooped down to his level. "What do you want to do?"

"Mama. Want Mama," he said.

The little boy kept looking back toward the entrance and she couldn't even guess how much he'd comprehended. She'd picked him up a cookie, but he wasn't interested in food. In fact, she thought she should probably take him out of this place.

"She was in an accident," Amelia said.

He put his thumb in his mouth and she sat down on the ground, lifting him onto her lap. She only knew one song that was even close to a lullaby and that was 'Bye Bye Blackbird.' Her mom used to sing it to her when she couldn't go to sleep so she cuddled Lane on her lap and sang it to him.

He put his head on her shoulder, the little Stetson on his head hitting her in the chin. This little cowboy was doing his best to be strong, but she could see he was scared and maybe a little tired. She hugged him closer to her and kept singing.

Her mom walked over to them, putting her hand on Amelia's shoulder, and started singing too. Lane's eyes got a little heavier. Amelia looked up at her mom, realizing how much she wished she could have the last thirteen years back. There it was. The reason she hadn't left modeling and come back home for good—she'd been unsure of how to move on, past the truth that was her life.

When they finished singing, her mom wobbled and Amelia lifted her hand to steady her, looking around for her father or sisters. But her mom just drew out a chair from the table and sat down on it.

"Are you okay?"

"As fine as I can be. Don't worry about me," Lilly said. "This little one needs our attention."

"That was the only song I knew. I don't know what else to do," she said.

"He just needs us to keep him busy," Mom said. "I'm sure whoever brought him to the party had a diaper bag with some toys and whatnot in it...but I don't see it. Do you see Emma's bag?"

"Over on the chair. Why?" Amelia asked, but she suspected her mom had an idea.

"Your sister always has either a tablet or e-reader with her. I'm hoping she's still using that mini tablet your father and I gave her for Christmas."

Lilly got up, steadied herself and then moved slowly through the party area to get Emma's bag. Lane tipped his head back, his hat falling on the ground next to them. She watched her mom, ready to go after her if she needed help, but Lilly was moving more easily now.

"Who you?"

"I'm Amelia. I'm a good friend of your uncle Cal's," she said. Good friend? Yeah, right. But today she was. "I knew him when he was just a boy."

"Unca Cal was little?"

"He was. Once, he was just like you," Amelia said.

Was she talking too much? She had no idea what a boy of his age would understand.

"Mela, where Mama?" he asked her as he looked down at his hands. She hugged him closer to her.

What was she going to say? Her heart was breaking for this little boy who'd lost his mother. And though her mom was still alive, a part of her identified with Lane. This was how she'd felt when she'd learned the truth all those years ago. It had been as if she'd had something ripped from her.

"Oh, baby, I'm not sure," Amelia said. This was definitely not the kind of news that she should deliver. She just hugged him close. "There was a bad accident. So, we're going to have to wait to find out."

"Found it!" her mom said, dropping down next to her and Lane on the grass. Her mom leaned in close. "What's the matter?"

"He asked me where his mama was," Amelia said.

Her mom reached over and brushed the white-blond hair off the little boy's forehead. "She was in an accident. That's why we are watching you so that she can get the help she needs."

He stuck his thumb back in his mouth and settled more fully on Amelia's lap. "I'll leave you two to play. There's a farm game on here that you'll both enjoy."

"Are you sure you're okay to go off by yourself?" she asked.

"I'm fine," her mom said, her mouth tight. She easily unlocked the mini tablet. She and her sisters all used their birthdays as their codes; they all could access each other's devices.

Her mom tapped on a farm game that Emma was obsessed with and handed the device to Amelia since Lane still sat on her lap. Amelia showed the little boy how to harvest a crop and then plant new ones. Then she turned on the sound because each animal and plant made a little noise.

"I'll go see what I can find out," her mom said. "You got this?"

"Yeah, I do," she said, catching her mom's wrist before she turned away. "Thanks, Mom."

"For what?"

"Just being you," she said.

Her mom kissed her on the forehead before walking away. The accident, seeing Cal and his brothers facing their new reality, drove home how fragile life was. She was holding on to anger and to the past because it seemed like she'd have forever to sort it out. And as petty as she knew it was, she wanted her mom to hurt as much as she had when she'd learned the truth.

THE CORBYN MANSION had always been on Ash and Main directly across from the bank. While other families had moved to ranches or to Austin or Houston, the Corbyns had stayed in their big house, updating and expanding it as the years went by. The sprawling Victorian mansion always looked warm and welcoming to her. She held Lane in her arms—the little boy had fallen asleep and Delilah, who'd had to go to the Dragonfly for the dinner service, had stopped by to tell her that all of the Delaneys had gone with Rose's body. So it looked like she'd be watching this little one for a bit longer. She liked it because it gave her something to focus on and she could go spend time at her parents' house without having to talk about the past.

And the Carriage House staff had started cleaning up so she'd figured it was time to go. She wasn't sure how long they would be and honestly, nothing in her life had prepared her for this kind of thing. Her grandmother opened the front door as Amelia was standing on the sidewalk just looking at the house.

"Come on up here. Your mom has made a place for this little one to sleep."

Amelia walked into the house—it smelled like it always did in spring. Gardenias. Her mother's favorite scent. For the first few years she'd been in New York, she'd avoided anything that had that scent. Today had changed something deep inside of her. And that ball of anger and hurt that she'd held on to for so long felt like it was loosening.

She carried Lane into the family room where her parents and Emma were sitting and quietly talking. Memaw nodded toward her father's recliner.

She saw that the chair had been fully reclined with a pillow, blanket and Mr. Stuffing. The stuffed bear had been in their family forever.

She tucked Lane under the blanket and carefully removed his boots. She recognized them as being made by Kelly Boots in neighboring Whiskey River.

"I don't have Cal's number. Has anyone heard from him?" Amelia asked.

"I've got it. I'll text him," Jasper said.

Her dad wasn't always a quick adapter to technology and a text from Jasper was like receiving a letter. He always addressed the recipient and used proper punctuation. She and her sisters teased him about it, but it was just the way he was.

Amelia plopped down on the couch next to Emma, who was reading. She glanced down at the book in her sister's lap and saw it was *The Scarlet Pimpernel*. Her sister loved that book series. Actually, she loved many books, which was why being a librarian was perfect for her.

Emma shifted until she was leaning against Amelia's shoulder and she put her arm around her little sister as she had so many times in the past. No one was talking, Louis Armstrong was playing quietly in the background and she closed her eyes for a moment. This was something she hadn't allowed herself to miss. Just sitting in the family room with her family.

"I need a drink," her mom said, going over to the bar cart. "Girls? Priscilla? Care to join me? Jasper mixed up some martinis earlier."

"Yes, please," Amelia said, thinking they all needed one

but at the same time, wondering if her mom should indulge. She glanced at Emma, who just shook her head.

"Definitely," Priscilla answered. "I might need two after today. That was so sad. I could hardly stand to see the destruction and, of course, the tragic deaths."

"Me either, Memaw," Emma said, getting up and going over to help their mom hand out the drinks before coming and sitting back down next to Amelia.

They all sipped their martinis, which her father made extra dry, just the way she liked them. She had resisted coming to these kinds of get-togethers since she'd been home but today, she was here and taking comfort in being part of the family. It was one of the things that she'd denied herself. When she was in New York, she didn't miss it but being back here just drove home the point that she might have been spiting herself trying to make her mom hurt.

"That little one looks so innocent, sleeping over there," Memaw said. "But he's sure seen a lot in his life."

"Memaw, isn't that being a touch melodramatic?"

"Not really, honey," her mom said, sitting down on Emma's other side on the large overstuffed leather couch. "Cal came home from the NFL when Rose got pregnant and there was a big blowup between them. He didn't want her to...well, he wanted her to finish school and go to college. But you know that his middle brother, Finn, dropped out to race in NASCAR. He got his GED, but still Rose didn't let Cal forget that there were a different set of rules for her."

Seemed like Cal had had a rough few years. But when she'd chatted with him, none of that had shown. He'd been the same cocky and confident Cal she'd always known. One of the things she'd envied about him when they were kids was how he'd just ignore the not-so-nice parts of his family life and walk around like everything was okay. It was one of the things she'd always struggled with.

She wasn't one of those people who could smile when she felt like crying or yelling. Her dad said she didn't have a poker face and her memaw thought it was that she just "felt" things too strongly. Delilah, on the other hand, just said she had no capacity for lying.

Amelia knew that was it. That one lie that had shaped her had burned it out of her. And sure, she'd lost some modeling gigs because she wouldn't put up with some guy touching her inappropriately, but she didn't care. She wasn't going to pretend something was okay when it wasn't. She'd modeled for some high-profile clients, including a famous cosmetics brand because her features were exotic-looking, and she'd loved that for a while. But in the end, it had all been empty. She didn't love it. It had just been something she'd used to escape, a way to hurt her mom the way Amelia had been hurt.

She'd realized that the lesson had made her grateful to her parents. She'd needed it when she'd left to go into a world where lies were the currency. Because she'd seen firsthand what it felt like to lose everything, she'd never felt the stakes were high enough for her to fudge the truth.

"Those boys will raise him. They are good at sticking together and taking care of each other," Jasper said. "It's going to be hard because Cal's been trying to raise not only

47

Rose, but also TJ and little Lane since he was born. But a child makes everyone stronger and gives life focus."

HIS BROTHERS WERE sitting in the pickup truck when he walked away from the medical facility. He could remember a number of times, when he'd barely been a legal driver, that he'd had to take the boys or Rose there. Rose. His heart pounded as he thought of her and it felt like he had rocks in his stomach. No matter how this felt like the past, it wasn't.

He wasn't out searching surrounding towns and bars for their father. He was walking back to his brothers after having seen their baby sister and her boyfriend in a morgue. They'd been inside with him for most of it, but Finn had cracked and walked out. He'd sent Braden after him.

There was no need for his brothers to wait to sign paperwork when he could do it on his own.

He shoved his hands into his hair. It felt grimy from the smoke earlier and he was starting to feel the soot and grime on his body. As he approached the truck, he noticed his brothers were deep in conversation. He didn't want to talk. He wanted to get drunk and then physically beat something, then drink some more and keep doing it until he was exhausted.

No matter what anyone said, he knew that the fault for this accident was his. He'd pushed Rose, insisting she get her degree, insisting that TJ step up. Just insisting on too damned much. If he'd insisted she stay home with Lane, she'd be alive. If he'd let her and TJ just live on the ranch or even bought them a house in town, they'd have been fine.

Hell, maybe insisting hadn't been the way. But frankly, he didn't know any other way to communicate. It had worked on the playing field and it worked in business because Braden was there to smooth things over. But it sure as hell hadn't worked with his little sister.

Suddenly playing house didn't seem like a bad fate for her. At least, she'd be alive.

But he'd wanted better for her. And this was what his desire for her future had wrought.

"Cal, you okay?" Finn asked, opening the door to the cab of the truck.

"Yeah, just trying to get my head straight."

"Good luck with that. We can't. Listen, we need to go and get Lane," Finn said. "But I'm not in any mood to handle him tonight."

"Me either," Braden said. "What are we going to tell him—" Braden's voice broke.

"I'll handle it. Why don't you two go to the ranch and I'll meet you later?"

"No," Finn said.

"What do you mean, no?" Cal asked.

He could see Finn was spoiling for a fight. It was his middle brother's way of dealing with his emotions. Finn had always shoved them down deep and pretended they didn't exist.

Today, Cal was almost in the mood to give it to him. Then maybe he could feel something other than the pain of loss.

"Maybe one of those sacks you took back in your playing days did knock you stupid, but no is pretty much a basic word. It means I ain't doing it," Finn said, getting out of the truck and standing next to it with his arms crossed over his chest.

"Maybe that last crash you had knocked the sense out of you. I've got four inches on you, little brother, and fifty pounds."

"Back when you were playing it was muscle, but you've gone soft—"

"Stop it—" Braden got between the two of them. "You both want to go and beat the shit out of each other, fine. But not here. Not in the parking lot."

Cal shook his head to clear it and turned away from Braden. His youngest brother was right. He was always the calm head during a storm, the one who was the peacekeeper much like their mom. He was the only one. Even Rose would be fighting with them.

Oh, shit. He walked away from his brothers. If he didn't, he might start crying. He didn't want to feel right now. There was too much to deal with. But Braden was right. This wasn't the place.

"Let's go home," Braden said. "I think that Lane is at the Corbyns' house. I'm going to ask Jasper to keep him overnight. We can go home and drink and fight and do all the other things we can't do with a toddler in the house, and then tomorrow we'll pick him up."

He walked back to the truck. Braden got in the middle

seat and they all put their seat belts on. No one spoke a word as they drove back through Last Stand. It was the only way to get to the Delaney ranch. Past the Fuhrmann statue and the spot where Rose had died. Where TJ had died. What were they going to tell Lancey, TJ's sister? She already had enough on her plate. But now they were all going to have to sit down and figure out what to do with Lane.

TJ's sister was in the Marines, so the chance of her coming home to raise the boy was slim. Plus, he couldn't let Delaney be raised by someone else. What would Rose have wanted?

She might have wanted her son far away from him. He hated that she might have died hating him. He wouldn't have blamed her. He'd been an ass. Screamed at her as she'd walked out the door that his word was law. Like some kind of asshole.

And now she was gone.

He had to live with that. He had to live with the fact that his temper and his idea of what the Delaneys were going to be had led to this. He wanted them to be better than the outlaws who lived on the outskirts of town and had spent more time in jail than out of it. He knew that the Delaneys had always come through when the town needed them but Cal had always wanted to be more than that. He wanted to be like the Corbyns or the Highwaters or the McBrides— families that contributed something to Last Stand other than a bawdy story and a hint of fear.

Chapter Five

A MELIA STARTED HER day the same way she had been
since she returned home but for once she felt like she
had a purpose. Yesterday, she'd committed to helping her
mom and today she meant to find a way to bring up the
things she wanted to discuss. Jax Williams, her biological
father, had never contacted her again after she'd helped him,
after the bone marrow transplant had been successful. So she
hadn't felt like there'd been another chance for her to talk
about it with anyone.

Her grandmother had always been there and willing to
talk but Amelia had needed to figure it out on her own.
Memaw seemed to understand that.

Maybe if she hadn't moved away…but she had.

She pulled up in front of her family home and noticed an
unfamiliar truck parked in the big driveway. She saw that
Stella, her mom's housekeeper, had parked her car in her
usual spot and the door to her dad's shed was open. She
thought about Lane, that poor little boy who'd lost both of
his parents and then she thought a bit more about how she'd
lost hers…because of her own actions.

Jasper and Lilly didn't ostracize her. No, she'd done it to

herself and had never figured out how to get back to where they'd been before she'd known the truth.

She shook her head. No use in dwelling on the past. How many times had her memaw or even Minna suggested that to her when she talked to them?

The full skirt of her cap-sleeved dress blew around her legs as she walked up the drive to her parents' front door. It was a gorgeous spring Monday, belying the tragedy of the day before. She'd always sort of thought that weather should reflect mood like it did in movies and books sometimes. But that wasn't reality.

The door opened as she got there and Cal stepped out, holding his sleeping nephew. She smiled at them both when he noticed her. He looked tired and drained. She'd never seen him this way before and she wished she knew something she could do or say to make this time easier for him. But she was at a loss.

"Morning, Cal," she said.

"Hiya, Amelia. Thank you for taking care of Lane yesterday," he said.

"You're welcome," she said, giving him a hug. "I'm so sorry for your loss. Is there anything I can do?"

"I don't think so," Cal said. "We haven't had a chance to plan anything."

"I'm going to bring food out there for dinner tonight," she said. "Is that okay?"

"Yeah," he said, nodding sort of vaguely. She suddenly realized that he was sleepwalking through this day. He wasn't ready to be back in his routine. Not yet.

Lane was curled in his arms and she noticed that Cal rubbed his nephew's back as he stood there watching her. She remembered something that her dad had said when Grandpa Joe had died, and Memaw was pretty much losing her mind. He'd told her and her sisters to keep her grandmother busy. She was willing to be that work for Cal too.

"What are you doing today?" she asked.

"I have to do some stuff in the office," he said vaguely.

"It's hard to picture you in an office," she admitted. "Whenever I think about you, it's always on the playing field."

"Well, that was when we used to hang out," he said. "But a lot of time has passed since then."

"It has. I'd love the chance to get to know you now," she said. She hadn't intended to say that, but it was truth.

"Hi, Mela," Lane said, rubbing his sleepy eyes and looking over at her.

"Hi, cutie. Did you sleep good?"

He nodded and when he did, she noticed that Mr. Stuffing was in his arms. Her dad's childhood bear. She was touched, and she knew her family would encourage her to help the Delaneys. It was the least she could do. Lane was wearing a Last Stand, Texas, T-shirt and a pair of shorts. She had no idea where her parents had found them.

"Do you want to play hooky today?" she asked Cal. There had never been a man who looked more…lost to her than Cal.

"Why?" he asked.

"Memaw's blackberry bushes are full of ripe fruit and I

have my great-grandmother's blackberry jam recipe..."

He tipped his head to the side, studying her with that dark gaze of his and she felt like he could see through her—that he knew she liked him, and he was one of the wrongs she was back in town to right.

"Sounds like fun. What do you say, Lane? Want to pick blackberries?"

"Sure," he said.

She smiled at them both. "Um, do you know where Memaw's house is?"

"Everyone does."

"I was going to walk over, but if you want to drive, I can meet you there. I have to go talk to my parents."

"We'll meet you there. We were heading to Kolalches for some donuts this morning. Can we bring you one?"

"Yes, please. Boston cream," she said.

He nodded and she turned away, walking up to her parents' front door. Cal Delaney. She knew that she should leave well enough alone. But he was going through something and of all the people in the world who had walked through her life, he was the one she felt she still owed something to. He'd stayed that sweet boy, her first love, locked in her memories all this time. And she couldn't just walk away from him when he was hurting.

Her mom was waiting in the foyer when she came in to the house. She was looking a little more tired than usual and Amelia debated if she should stay and talk, but honestly, she wasn't ready to. Seeing Lane, knowing how lost he was stirred something inside of her. She wanted to be there for that little boy.

"Can you manage the shop without me today?" Amelia said.

"Yes, I can. I think those two need you more than I do," Mom said. "What's going on there?"

"We're just old friends. But he seemed like he could use someone today," she said.

"I couldn't agree more," her mom said. "Enjoy your day and maybe tonight, you can come by for dinner."

"I promised to bring something out to the Delaneys."

"Good idea. I'll bake a casserole, too," Mom said. "So tomorrow for breakfast?"

She knew her mom wasn't going to let her wiggle out of talking alone, just the two of them. She sighed and nodded. "Why don't you come to my place? I'll cook."

KOLACHES WAS BUSY as he walked in and Lane squirmed to get down. He wore his boots and a pair of shorts and a T-shirt that the Corbyns had rustled up for him and his Stetson, which he took off when they entered the building, the same as Cal did. He ruffled his little nephew's hair as they waited. Slowly as people started to recognize them, they either turned away or came over and offered their condolences.

Shane Highwater hadn't released the accident report, but it didn't take a trained investigator to recognize that Rose had run the light. His skin started to feel like it was too tight for his body again. If Lane hadn't been over at the glass case staring at all of the pastries, Cal would have walked out of the bakery.

He wasn't ready to talk to anyone in town. Not even the well-meaning people.

Someone slipped their arm around his shoulder and he glanced over to see that it was Delilah. "Dude, you looked like you were about to go psycho killer."

"I am. I am so not ready for this," he admitted.

"Yeah, why don't you chill outside," Delilah said. "Pretend to be on your phone. I'll get your order. What do you want?"

He shook his head. That smacked of cowardice. He could stand in a line and order pastries without wigging out. It wasn't like Rose was waiting for him. Again, he felt that mélange of emotions roiling through him and he knew with absolute certainty that he was going to lose it.

"Whatever you get will be fine," he said, handing Delilah his wallet. "Your sister wants a Boston cream."

"Got it."

He walked outside to the jingle of the bell, pulled his sunglasses out of his front pocket and went to lean against the building. Taking Delilah's advice, he pulled his phone out of his pocket and glanced down at the screen.

Dammit.

The lock screen had a reminder that he was supposed to meet TJ at the bank this afternoon.

He rubbed the back of his neck. Lancey hadn't called them yet but he knew she'd been on a weekend pass and had to get back to base. He had to get in touch with her and the family lawyer was coming out this afternoon to talk about custody of Lane. He really had no business picking blackberries this morning.

The scent of lavender drifted to him on the wind and he looked up to see Amelia walking toward him. She leaned against the building next to him, her long legs crossed at the ankles. "Do you want to skip blackberry picking and just go home?"

He looked at her, feeling like his emotions were hidden by the barrier of his dark aviator-style sunglasses. Go home?

No.

No matter where he went, he was faced with the truth that Rose was gone. And he couldn't escape it or find a path to peace. Of course, it had been one day.

"Does it get easier?" he wondered out loud.

"Yes, but not for a long time," she said.

"How do you know?"

"Just based on losing Grandpa Joe, and when I left Last Stand."

He tilted his head toward her and then looked away. "How does that compare?"

"I felt like I'd lost my home. That I wasn't going to ever have it back. The first few months when I was in New York, I reached for the phone to call and ask if I could come back but stopped myself when I remembered the truth."

"What truth?" he asked. Actually, this was the distraction he needed. "You were a teenager who had a great family and good friends. What secret could have driven you away?"

She chewed her lower lip between her teeth. Before she could answer, the door opened and Delilah came out holding a bag in one hand and carrying his nephew on her back.

"This little cowboy said he needed a piggyback ride," Delilah said, her long blond hair cascading down her back and over his nephew who was wearing the biggest smile that Cal had seen on him in a while.

For a few moments, he'd forgotten about his mama and Cal was glad. Lane would never forget Rose. They'd make sure of it. But he didn't want his nephew to grow up in the specter of sadness and grief.

Amelia grabbed the bag from her sister and Delilah stooped down to let Lane get off her back. "Remember what I said about not eating too many blackberries, scamp."

She stood back up. "If you have some extras, bring them by the restaurant. I'd love to use them in a dish I'm working on."

"I will. Thanks for this," Amelia said lifting up the bag.

"Thank Cal. It was his treat," she said, handing him back his wallet.

Delilah hugged her sister, ruffled Lane's hair and then hugged him before walking away. They all watched her leave.

"I know the best place to eat breakfast," Amelia said to Lane, taking his hand in hers. "A big swing under an arbor of rose bushes."

"Like Mama."

"Just like Mama," Amelia said, and Cal felt his throat get tight. He wasn't going to be able to do this. Not today.

Maybe not ever. There was too much inside of him and all the tequila in the world hadn't dulled it.

"I can't do this," he said.

"Okay," she said. "How about if you come home with me so you don't have to be alone?"

"Okay."

CAL JUST STARTED walking up Main toward the cross street that led to her grandmother's house. She followed along with Lane, thinking that she was the worst person in the world to be trying to help him. She wasn't good at dealing with emotion. She ran away when things got too dicey—she knew that and so did Cal. *Firsthand.*

But she wasn't running this time. When she'd come back to Last Stand, she'd made a promise to herself and she was determined to keep it. No more taking off. No more avoiding the uncomfortable things.

Lane walked slowly and took his time stopping to pick a stick up off the ground and then he took his hat off and straightened it out.

Cal stopped and turned back and she saw a man...so broken. She knew she needed to make today about fun and keep Lane occupied so Cal could deal with everything he had going on.

She didn't think about it, she knew what she had to do. So she scooped Lane up in her arms and went to Cal, wrapped him in her arms and just held him. "This sucks.

This is always going to suck and I wish you weren't in this position."

His arms came around her and he held her and Lane tightly to him, his face buried in her neck. She felt the burn of his tears against her collarbone. She just held him.

"Unca, don't be sad," Lane said, and Amelia saw his little hand patting Cal's shoulder.

Cal rubbed his eyes against her shoulder and lifted his head, taking Lane from her. And then he held her hand as they continued walking toward Memaw's house. She fell into step beside him and when they got to her grandmother's home, they went around back to the converted carport. Memaw's car wasn't there—she had Bible study first thing in the morning.

So they went to the carport with the large swinging bed that was draped with a spring patterned quilt that Memaw and Great-Aunt Edie had made when they were girls. Lane was pretty excited to see a bed that was a swing and Cal sat down on it with his nephew.

"Chocolate milk for Lane? Or juice? Coffee for us?" she asked.

"Apple juice for Lane," Cal said. "He needs a straw."

"I got you covered. You guys see if you can get that swing working. I'll be back soon," she said. Then she took the path that led to the back door of her memaw's house and keyed in the code to unlock the door.

Christy, her grandmother's rescue collie, came running over to greet her, she rubbed the dog's neck and gave her a treat before she went to make cups of coffee for herself and

Cal and fix the juice for Lane.

She added a splash of fat-free half-and-half to her coffee and realized she didn't know how Cal took his. She started to lean out the back door to ask him and saw him sitting in the middle of the bed swing, holding Lane, his head bent over his nephew's. They were talking quietly and she realized he might need some time alone with his sister's son.

So, she sat down at the kitchen table where she had a view of Cal and drank her coffee. She was stumbling her way through this and she wasn't going to try to stick to a schedule or make him do anything he wasn't ready for.

It was clear to her he needed time and space. And this place that wasn't his home. A place where he'd never seen Rose and wouldn't be surrounded by her memories.

She pulled out her phone and answered a few emails while she gave him his privacy and then she looked up and noticed he was looking at the house. There was something about Cal that made it hard for her to keep her attention on what she was doing. Her gaze kept straying back to him. It didn't help that he looked even better now than he had in high school. She knew he needed a friend and she wanted to be that to him.

"Hey," she said, opening the back door so she had a reason to see him. "I don't know how you take your coffee."

"Milk and two sugars," he said with a smile that made her notice how full his mouth was.

She nodded and went to make it the way he'd requested. "Just be his friend," she muttered to herself.

Then she walked back outside and they had their breakfast with very little conversation. After they'd cleaned up, she gathered some baskets from the bar area on the carport.

Lane stood next to Cal and she was impressed watching him interact with his nephew. But she knew she shouldn't be. Cal had always had a natural way with people. He was patient with Lane and helped him carefully pick the berries and when they had filled up their baskets, he looked over at her. She had never thought of herself as maternal but when she looked at Lane, she wanted to hold him close and keep him safe forever.

"Thank you."

"For?" she asked, trying to play it cool.

"This. I did need to be outside," he admitted.

"I'm glad. I owe you so much more than I can ever repay you, Cal," she admitted. She'd sort of used him in a way that she knew wasn't fair. But he had been the only person she'd felt she could be herself with.

"I think we should let the past die," he said. "Maybe figure out a way to move forward."

"As friends, right?"

He quirked one eyebrow at her. "If that's what you want."

She didn't know what she wanted. "I just like being around you. I'm not ready to talk about why I left but I want you to know that you brought me a lot of comfort when I was alone those first few years in New York City."

He nodded. "See, when you say things like that you confuse me. You always have and I wish there was some way I could just forget you and let you go. But there is a part of me that has always wanted you."

She knew that he didn't like wanting her but it made her heart feel lighter when he said that. She leaned in closer to him. Their eyes met and she felt a zing go through her. His lips when they brushed against hers were firm yet soft at the same time.

He put his hand on the side of her neck, his fingers tangling in her hair as she tipped her head to the side, deepening the kiss. He tasted better than she remembered. His kiss had a sophistication to it that he hadn't had when they'd been teens.

But the attraction that had been between them? That had been dormant all these years, but now, it sprang to life. She shivered, shifting closer to him, putting her hand on his chest as he thrust his tongue deep into her mouth.

She barely heard the sound of a car door closing but Cal pulled back. His lips were moist and swollen from their kiss. Her own were tingling and she rubbed her finger over them.

"That just reinforces my confusion."

Chapter Six

C AL TOOK LANE home, trying to forget about that kiss. He didn't know what had come over him. He wasn't in the market for a girlfriend and to be perfectly honest, even if he was, Amelia would be the last woman he'd consider. She had baggage and they had history.

He was a forward-looking guy.

Or so he'd always thought. He pulled under the wrought-iron sign that said 'The Delaneys' and drove straight to the newly remodeled ranch house. When he'd gotten his signing bonus with the NFL, the first thing he did was redo the house. Not just for Rose and Braden, who'd lived there full time, but because he wanted this to be a new era for his family.

No more fighting and robbing, no more curses and bad juju that they'd never been able to outrun. Their father, despite his drinking, had worked hard and provided for them. His brothers had careers, respectable ones, though some would argue both himself and Finn making their living playing games wasn't respectable. But he knew differently.

He pulled his pickup off to the side of the driveway and stared at the big house that had every fancy luxury Rose had wanted. And then, he just started sobbing. He couldn't help it. His heart was one big open wound at this moment. Lane slept quietly in his car seat and Cal was looking at the future and seeing that it was hollow, empty.

Kissing Amelia wasn't going to change that.

Nothing had…and nothing would. Pumping money into the local economy by starting Outlaw Tequila and training kids at the high school to work the vats under strict supervision. It was okay, but he was never going to do enough for his family not to be remembered as a bunch of outlaws.

The outlaws Delaney.

He wiped his eyes and started moving again. He had to know his boundaries. He'd tried, God knows that he had. But it was time to just be what he was. His generation wasn't going to be the one to break the curse. Maybe little Lane's would be.

He parked the car in front of the house and got his nephew out of the back seat. Mrs. Hanson's car was in the driveway. She was a forty-year-old woman whose daughter was Braden's assistant at Outlaw Tequila and she often helped them babysit Lane, as she had before the party. He noticed that Braden's car was in the driveway, but Finn's was gone.

It was probably a good thing—he was itching for a fight. Finn always was. His brother was never happy unless he was fighting or driving 300 miles an hour. Cal thought that was the only way Finn had learned to protect the vulnerability his middle brother liked to pretend he didn't have.

He carried Lane into the house, hearing the sound of

voices in the kitchen. Using the sleeping toddler as an excuse to avoid them, he went up the stairs to Lane's room. It was attached to Rose's, but he ignored that. Didn't even glance at the open door that led to her room.

He saw that she'd left out his pajamas on the changing table and a book. She'd always like to get things ready in the morning before she left. Damn.

He'd thought he could avoid this by coming upstairs but it wasn't helping.

He changed Lane and tucked him into his toddler bed that had a racecar frame. He kissed his nephew before making sure the nanny cam was on and logging into his app to check on him.

"Cal, is that you up there?" Braden called.

"Yes. Just putting Lane to bed. He's fast asleep," Cal said, knowing he was talking too much but unable to stem the flow of words.

The doorbell rang as he was coming down the stairs and Braden answered it. There was Amelia. She had changed clothes, and now wore a pair of jeans and sleeveless top.

"I made a casserole for you. It's Delilah's recipe so should be delicious," she said.

Cal stayed where he was on the stairs for a moment, just looking at her. Technically, she was one of the prettiest women he'd ever seen. She always took his breath away.

She noticed him coming down the stairs and smiled over at him and a jolt of lust went through him. Damn. He wanted her. Right now, he just needed someone to hold and to forget for a few hours.

He couldn't use her like that. They were neighbors of a sort and he respected her dad.

But another part of him thought, she was here and smiling at him… Why not just see what happened?

"Want to join us for dinner?" he asked, taking the casserole dish from her. It smelled delicious.

"If you don't mind the company, I'd love to stay," she said.

"It would probably be good for us to have someone else to talk to," Braden said. "Otherwise, I'll just talk shop."

"He's a crazy workaholic," Cal said, stepping back as Amelia entered the foyer and walked toward the kitchen.

Mrs. Hanson was in there, but she had her bag on her shoulder and her keys in her hand.

"I'm heading out now. I can come back tomorrow if you need me to watch Lane. But this weekend, I'm working at one of the charity booths at the Bluebonnet Festival."

"I'll text you once we know what we are doing with Lane tomorrow," Cal said, walking her out and then returning to the kitchen where Braden had set three places at the island.

Amelia was laughing at something his brother had said and he stood and watched her, wanted her. He didn't censor himself. He wasn't able to be civilized or play any kind of game right now.

She glanced up as Braden left the room and their eyes met, and he knew she could read his thoughts. They weren't that hard to decipher at this moment. Her lips parted, and she drew her tongue over them. He groaned.

But at that moment Braden came back into the kitchen

with three longneck bottles of beer and he turned away. He could wait until after they ate but if she looked at him like that again, he knew he'd be hard pressed to walk away.

AMELIA WAS THE first to admit that she still had no idea what she was doing at the Delaney ranch but she was having a good time with Braden and Cal. It had been a while since she'd associated anything good with her hometown. She had to admit that postponing coming home might not have been her smartest idea. Braden and Cal were funny together. Cal was taller and more muscular, bearing a distinct resemblance to his ancestors, whereas Braden looked more like his mother's people. Their temperaments were different too.

Braden had a dry sense of humor and didn't hesitate to needle his oldest brother. *A lot.* Which was fun to see because that one time she'd seen him in New York, he'd been very much the celebrity football player and everyone had treated him with a sort of deference.

She hadn't expected to run into him and his girlfriend at the United Way gala but there they had been. She had wanted to be all cool and sophisticated when she saw him but instead, she'd stared at him until her dinner partner had offered to introduce them. She hadn't realized the boy she'd known—and that was how she'd been thinking of Cal until that moment—had grown up and taken the world by storm.

"Thanks for this," Braden said, as he cleaned up the dishes. "I have some work to do, so if you don't mind, I'll say good night, Amelia."

"Not at all. I probably won't stay much longer," she said.

"I was hoping you'd stay for a bit," Cal said. "We never got to finish our conversation earlier."

She nodded. Yeah, the one where she explained why she'd ghosted him back in high school. She hadn't talked to anyone about it. Well, that wasn't technically true. She and her sisters had discussed it the night she'd found out. They'd sat on the floor of her walk-in closet, huddled close together, trying to make sense of the fact that she wasn't technically a Corbyn.

"I'd like to then," she said as Braden left. She got up and put the lid on her casserole dish and put it in the fridge while Cal put the dishes in the dishwasher. She was struck by how normal this was. And for a moment, she was glad she'd been able to give them this. She knew that life for the Delaney boys wasn't going to be normal for a while but little moments like this one would help.

"Want to sit on the front porch swing?" she suggested. Partly because it was a gorgeous April evening, but mostly because she didn't trust herself alone with Cal in the family room.

"Sure," he said. "Want another drink?"

"I can't. I'm driving," she said.

"Iced tea?"

"Yes, please," she said.

He poured two drinks and she looked around the house as he did it. "This place is really nice. I remember it from when we dated, but it seems you've done a lot of work to it."

"Yeah, totally gutted the house and redid everything. None of my ancestors had ever put any money into the ranch so it was definitely needed."

"It's nice."

"Thanks," he said, leading the way to the front porch.

She sat down on the swing and he sat next to her, kicking it into motion with the heel of his foot. She held her mason jar tea glass in her hands and tipped her head back to stare out at the open range around the Delaney house.

"So...you were going to tell me why you had to leave," he said.

"Yeah, I was," she said, turning to face him. She'd told a watered-down version of the truth to people before. She found that most people only asked about her past and why she'd left to move a conversation forward. She could usually distract them with easy things that they probably already assumed about her, like she'd discovered that small-town life wasn't big enough for her, that sort of thing. But Cal wasn't going to be fooled by that.

"You said it was complicated," he prompted.

"It is. Um, how much do you want to know?" she asked after a few moments.

"Whatever you want to tell me. You brought it up so obviously it's on your mind," he said. "Our past is just that—the past. But if it's something that is between us now, then we should deal with it."

"I don't remember you being a 'deal with it' kind of guy," she said. "You were always more of a 'let's do something physical' so I don't have to talk."

He laughed and she smiled.

"Yeah, well, when I played college ball, my coaches weren't big fans of me fighting things out. One of them was a real mentor to me. He told me that if you had a plan in place, every situation was winnable."

"Do you think that's true?" she asked. She had been in so many losing positions over the course of her life, ones where she'd had to brazen it out or just walk away.

"Most of the time. Having a plan, dealing with the awkward shit, that always makes it easier. Even when I used to fight with the guys, the problem would still be there the next day," he said.

"I like that. Well, um, actually the reason I left is the reason I came back. Something happened between me and my parents and I've never faced it, never been able to deal with it. But time is sort of running out, and my dad told me either come home and face it or regret it the rest of my life."

Cal arched one eyebrow at her as he stretched his arm along the back of the swing.

"That sounds a bit melodramatic for Jasper, but hey, he got you to come home."

She nodded. "He wasn't being dramatic. Mom has…Mom is sick. The doctors don't have a full diagnosis yet but they haven't ruled out Alzheimer's."

"I'm sorry to hear that. I didn't know," he said.

"Yeah, we're keeping it quiet until we know more," she said.

"So whatever it is, it's something you want to talk with her about before it's too late," he said.

"Yes, though it's something that you never want to talk to your parents about," she said, starting as vaguely as she could.

"I can think of a few things…sex, drugs, partying too much," he said.

"Yeah, that's about it," she said.

⸎

SHE WAS SO quiet about this. Given the way she'd brought it up and then retreated, he wondered if he should just let it go. But she wanted to talk…he could see it. He'd seen the signs in Rose and because he was her older brother, he'd never been able to listen. He'd always been too ready to tell her the right way to do something or try to caution her against making the same mistakes he had.

This was his chance to make up for that. And he'd be a gentleman. No noticing that her lipstick had worn off and the natural color of her lips was a rosy pink. No catching that super soft strand of hair that kept brushing against his wrist with his finger. He would be nothing but being a friend. He could do this.

Yeah, right, his libido said.

But he wasn't ruled by his dick.

Not tonight.

"Who partied like that? Your mom?" he asked. He couldn't see either Jasper or Mrs. Corbyn as wild party animals. Jasper Corbyn was born wearing ironed jeans and a button-down shirt. He could let loose on occasion but usually it was when he was sitting in his backyard drinking Wild Turkey and smoking a cigar.

"Yes, my mom," she said, drawing her leg up underneath her.

Well, hell, how was he supposed to not notice how long her legs were, now that she was canted toward him on the bench.

"What did she do?"

"Um, I feel silly saying this, but you can't tell anyone what I'm about to tell you," she said.

"Okay," he said. "I don't know what you think about me but I'm not really one to stand around talking about people in town."

She shook her head and put her hand on his shoulder. "I didn't mean it that way. Once you hear it, you'll understand."

He was starting to get a bit worried. Was her mom's health issue due to some sort of addiction? Having grown up with an alcoholic father, he understood what it was like to live with an addict.

"Is it drugs? Don't worry, whatever it is, I'm here for you. I won't talk to anyone about anything you share with me. I hated that everyone in town knew Dad was a drunk. It made it harder to pretend to be like everyone else."

She squeezed his shoulder again. "I know. I remember when he had to spend sixty days in the county lockup for drinking and driving. I told everyone who asked that he was home every night."

He smiled at her. "You were a good girlfriend, Ams.

Why did you leave like that? I know you well enough to realize you're stalling."

She sighed, pulling her hand from his and wrapping her own arms around her waist. She looked at her lap and then out at the sky, which was darkening with twilight. The landscape lights were coming on and the porch had an imitation flicking gaslight that came on as well.

"I found out that very afternoon that Jasper isn't my biological father."

He shook his head, not sure he'd heard that right. "What?"

"That was my reaction, too," she said.

"Why would they suddenly tell you that at sixteen?" he asked. "I'm shocked. I never saw anything about your family to make me think that Jasper wasn't your dad."

"Me either," she said. "They told me because... Do remember when Mom took me to Houston for that blood test?"

"I do because you were absent from school for two days," he said. She'd been his first serious girlfriend. So, everything had been so intense. When Amelia left, his father had told him that it was the Delaney curse and to remember that they weren't meant for a forever kind of love. And Cal had realized his father knew what he was talking about.

"Um, my biological father had contacted my mom because he had cleaned up his act and his girlfriend had a baby boy who was sick. He wasn't a match and he knew about me, so he got in contact. It turned out I was a bone marrow match for the baby and so my parents had to tell me the truth."

"Well, shit. That's a lot for anyone to take in. No wonder you wigged out," he said. It didn't justify the way she'd left but he understood it. He had never blamed her for leaving him—he knew there was more at play. He'd never guessed this though.

"Yeah, so I went and did the medical procedure for the baby. And then, you know I'd been scouted by a famous modeling agency but Mom and Dad had said no to me going to New York?"

He nodded.

"Well my biological dad owed me, and he paid for a place for me there. I told Mom I would run away if she didn't give her permission, so she did," Amelia said. "I was so freaked out, I couldn't even stay in the same room as her, and every time I saw my dad I burst into tears. So, I drove to your place. I was going to ask you go come with me, but you told me about the college scouts coming to practice and I thought about your life with your brothers and Rose and I knew that you were meant to stay here."

He understood that. He didn't know what he would have done if she'd asked him to leave. He was glad he hadn't had to make that decision. "There's one thing I don't understand. I asked you before but I don't think you told me the real reason."

"What's that?" she asked.

"I get that you were leaving, but you'd been pretty adamant that we weren't going to hook up. But then, that night...why did you want to?"

She took a deep breath but didn't say anything for a long time.

"I wanted my first time to be with someone I cared about. Everything else in my world was changing and I wanted a little bit of you to take with me."

Chapter Seven

S HE KNEW IT hadn't been fair to put that on him, but she wanted him to know that she hadn't used him…well, that she hadn't used him without a good reason. She had cared a lot for Cal as only a sixteen-year-old could, but she'd always been angry, stubborn and determined to make her own path.

He was watching her with an expression that she couldn't read and maybe that was a good thing. Maybe it was better that she didn't know what was on his mind. It wasn't as if there was anything good he could say.

The swing stopped moving and she realized that she might have ruined any hope of a second chance with him by admitting the truth of her emotions back then, but because of what had happened with her parents, she couldn't tolerate lying. Even when she knew it would be better to keep something to herself.

"So, yeah, I guess I should be going," she said. He might need time to think about what she'd said or maybe he'd already decided that she wasn't worth his time.

She started to stand up but he caught her hand, tugging her back down onto his lap. The swing bounced as she landed on him with more force than she'd expected.

"I can't make up my mind if I'm flattered or not that you wanted your first time to be with me," he said. "I mean, of course, you know that night was my first time, too. I thought—well it doesn't matter. That night has always been tinged by the next morning. By you not coming to school and then learning from your sister that you'd left Last Stand."

Shame over her actions rolled through her. She hadn't meant to hurt him. The memory of Cal had been one of the best parts of her new life. Having him in her mind had soothed her when she'd been scared.

"I am sorry," she said. "Sorrier than you will ever know. If I'd been older, I hope I would have reacted differently, maybe been smart enough not to sleep with you. Maybe I would have been able to consider the impact on you. But I didn't. I was so hurt and scared and you were a comfort."

"Comfort?" he asked. "That's how you think of our night together."

Their eyes met, and she saw the humor on his face. "Yeah. I mean, of course it was totally awesome too."

"You're making it worse," he said, shifting her around so that her feet rested on the bench of the swing and she nestled in his arms against his chest.

"How can I make it up to you?" she asked. "I owe you."

"You don't owe me. That night was incredible," he said. "We don't owe each other anything."

"Are you sure?" she asked.

"Yes, I am. At the time, I was pissed off but it's been like what—thirteen years? I think I can let it go now," he said.

"Thank you," she said.

"So, what did your mom say to make you so mad?" he asked.

There was no way to explain her behavior of the last thirteen years without revealing how bratty she'd been. And truthfully, she wasn't sure she wanted to talk about that time. Cal already had enough on his mind with his sister. Maybe she could help him. Maybe he needed something from her, the way she had needed him all those years ago.

"Nothing. She and Dad told me what had happened. I know I should probably refer to him as Jasper but I can't. He'll always be Dad to me."

"That makes sense," Cal said, pushing the swing in motion again. "He's just a solid kind of guy. We sort of bonded after you'd left. I went to your house after school, but no one was home so I went to the bank... I was really worried that something had happened to you. Anyway, Jasper invited me into his office, said you'd gone to New York to model. That things had happened in your family that had upset you.

"I must have looked like I was confused and hurt because he told me that you were running from something that scared you. And he was sure you didn't want to leave me."

A wave of love for her dad went through her. "That's so him. He's just a nice guy. I mean I could see why Mom would want to be with him."

"How did it happen?"

"Um, Mom had been to a Jax Williams concert two days before her first date with Dad. Memaw had conspired with

Granny Nadine to set them up on a date, but Mom said they were both so different that neither expected anything to come of it. Jax had been performing in Luckenbach and it was a small and close setting. They met, and she said...he had a certain charm. One thing led to another and they hooked up. She said that it hadn't been love, just a one-night thing."

He rubbed his hands up and down her arms. She realized as she was talking just how much of her past she still resented. "That almost makes it worse in a way. I mean I am the product of a hookup."

He tipped her chin back and their eyes met. "You aren't. Jasper Corbyn and your mom wanted you. They made a family around you and I think that's pretty special."

His spin on her past made her feel special, though she knew she wasn't. But she realized that Cal had a gift for taking the ordinary and making it seem...like magic.

She didn't want to talk about her past anymore or think about it. She was in Cal's arms—the one place she'd never thought she'd be again. And tonight, it felt like it was just the two of them and the big Texas sky. That nothing else existed. Not the pain that had plagued both of them over the past thirteen years, not the horrible tragedy that had occurred just yesterday. Tonight was all about the two of them and the lusty attraction that time hadn't dulled.

She put her hands on either side of his jaw, feeling the abrasiveness of his stubble against her palms as she drew his head down toward hers. Their lips met and she knew that it hadn't been a fluke earlier in Memaw's garden. The passion was still there.

HOLDING AMELIA IN his arms made the grief inside him almost tolerable. For a few minutes, it wasn't consuming him. And he was willing to do whatever he had to in order to keep it at bay. The things she'd told him about her past made his heart ache for the young girl she'd been.

While she hadn't been perfect, she had been special. He knew how much being a Corbyn girl had meant to her. And while to him she'd always be one, he could see how it was different for her.

But that wasn't why he kept kissing her. He wanted everything she had to give him. He wanted to make love to her again so that he could prove to himself it hadn't been just a fluke. And so he could forget everything else. Amelia had always sort of consumed him.

That hadn't changed in thirteen years.

He lifted his head and looked down at her face. Her eyes were closed, her cheeks in the flickering lamplight were flushed, her lips wet from their kiss and slightly swollen. Cupping the back of her neck, he rubbed his finger up and down the column of her neck until her eyes opened. Their gazes met, and he felt something primal spring to life inside of him. The calmness he'd been carefully cultivating since he'd sat next to her on the swing was gone.

He didn't like the way it swamped him or how out of control he felt.

She touched her finger to his lips and he groaned. He couldn't help it. He was on the edge and everything she did further enflamed him. He wasn't going to be able to walk away.

"Do you want me?" he asked, carefully. "We hardly know each other now."

"That doesn't matter. I feel like I've always known you, Cal. I do want you," she said. "But I know the timing isn't right."

"When is it going to be right?" he asked. "One thing Rose's accident—" He stopped speaking as his voice cracked.

She pulled him into her arms. "What can I do? I know that there is nothing to stop you from thinking about her. Do you want to talk about her?"

"Talking…I don't think I can," he said, his voice breaking. "I keep expecting her to walk back in the door. Even Braden can't stand to be around right now. Yet it's Lane's home."

She held him close to her, moving around until they were lying next to each other. He didn't know how to ask for comfort. Wasn't even sure he deserved it. But she seemed to understand.

She leaned up to kiss him. He guessed she meant to offer him some comfort, but he needed something more. He deepened the kiss, his tongue brushing over hers as he skimmed his hands over her back, rolling so that she was on top of him. As she settled over his hips, his erection stirred and grew beneath her.

He knew he should walk away. He wasn't really in any

position to be making love to Amelia—not now—but she framed his face with her hands again, and he realized how much he liked it when she touched him. She rested her forehead against his and he felt the brush of her long hair against his shoulder.

He caught her wrists in his hands and drew them back behind her, so that her spine arched, and her breasts were thrust toward him. Her long hair fell forward, curling over the top of her right breast. Her ebony-colored hair contrasted with the paleness of her skin, as he slowly removed her blouse and bra.

When he'd finished, she tugged her wrists free and reached for his shirt buttons. Blood rushed through his veins, pooling in his groin and hardening him even more as she slowly unbuttoned his shirt. Her fingers were cool against his skin as she worked her way down his body. When she finished, she pushed it open, scraping her nails down his chest and squeezing his pecs.

He shrugged out of his shirt and tossed it aside. He growled deep in his throat as he felt her breath against his chest and then the brush of her lips. Nibbling her way from one collarbone to the other, he felt the edge of her teeth as she grazed his skin.

He watched her kissing him, touching him, and got even harder in his jeans, which were getting to be too tight. Her tongue darted out and brushed against his nipple. His hips jerked forward as he put his hand on the back of her head, urging her to continue kissing him.

"Where did you get this?" she asked, her tongue tracing

over the scar tissue on his left shoulder. He normally wasn't much of a talker during sex, but he would do anything to make this last longer. Draw it out so he didn't get sucked back into the real world.

"That's where I had my surgery after I got sacked. The defensive lineman caught me midthrow and it wrenched my shoulder out of its socket. It took several surgeries to regain flexibility in it."

"God, that must have been really painful," she said. She had one hand braced on his chest as she leaned over him.

He shifted under her and lifted her in his arms so that she straddled him. He leaned up and kissed her lips. "At the time, I was more concerned about not being able to play anymore. But it did hurt, and physical therapy was a bitch too."

"I'm sorry," she said, rubbing her fingers lightly over the scar and then kissing it.

He rubbed his hands over the length of her naked back, enjoying the feel of Amelia in his arms. And as desperate as he was to be inside of her, this was nice too.

She put her hands on his shoulders and eased her way down his chest. Moving as if they had all night, she traced each of the muscles that ribbed his abdomen. He'd continued working out even though his playing days were over. He found that physical activity took the edge off his restlessness most days and he was glad now that he had.

She was enjoying his body and that made his chest swell and his shoulders sit a bit straighter. As she moved lower, her fingers feathering down toward the button fly of his jeans, he stopped breathing. He felt his heartbeat in his erection where it was pressed against the fly of his jeans. As she reached the edge of his pants, she stopped and glanced up his body to his face.

He nodded and sort of grunted. Words beyond him at the moment. She just smiled, which made him groan again, her hand going to his erection, brushing over his straining length.

He lifted her slightly so that her nipples brushed his chest.

She nibbled on her lips as he rotated his shoulders so that his chest rubbed against her breasts. His blood roared in his ears and he couldn't see anything but her naked in his arms. But they both still wore their jeans and he was so hard, so full right now that he needed to be inside of her body.

Impatient with her clothes, he stood up and set her on her feet as he undid her jeans and then shoved them down her legs.

She laughed and stepped out of the flip-flops she'd worn on her feet and then out of her jeans. He caressed her long, lean thighs. God, she was soft. She moaned as he neared her center and then sighed when he brushed his fingertips across the crotch of her panties.

The lace was warm and wet. He slipped one finger under the material and hesitated for a second, looking up into her electric-blue eyes.

She bit down on her lower lip and he felt the minute movements of her hips as she tried to move his touch where she needed it. Pushing the fabric of her panties aside, he delicately outlined the opening of her body. She was warm and wet and so ready for him. It was only the fact that he wanted her to climax at least once before he took her that enabled him to keep his own needs in check.

She shifted against him and he entered her body with just the tip of one finger. He teased them both with a few short thrusts.

"Cal…" she said, her voice breathless and airy.

"Yes, darlin'?"

"I need more than you teasing me."

He pushed his finger further up into her body. "How's this?"

"Good," she moaned as her hips rocked against his finger for a few strokes.

He removed his finger and traced it around her clit. She bit her lower lip and let her head fall back as she drove her hips frantically against him.

He undid his own jeans and freed his cock before lifting her off her feet and sitting back down on the swing. Straddling him again, he felt the brush of his naked cock against her warm center and he cursed.

"I don't have a condom," he said, between gritted teeth.

"I'm on the pill," she said. "And healthy."

"Hell, yeah."

She kissed him, thrusting her tongue deep into his mouth as she leaned forward, bracing her hands on his shoulders. Her breasts brushed his chest, her nipples now tight little nubs.

He lowered his head, taking her beaded nipple into his

mouth and suckling her deeply. As he traced his fingers down the side of her body, he nipped at her waist and then moved his hand lower, to her pussy. He plunged two fingers into her body. He kept his thumb on her clit as he worked his fingers deep inside her, and within minutes, she threw her head back and called his name.

He felt the tightening of her body against his fingers. She kept rocking against him for a few more minutes and then collapsed against him. She turned her head until their mouths met and tangled her hands in the back of his hair. Her nails dug into his shoulders and she leaned up, brushing against his chest. Her nipples were hard points and he pulled away from her mouth, glancing down to see them pushing against his chest.

He caressed her back and spine, scraping his nail down the length of it. He followed the line of her back down the indentation above her backside. She closed her eyes and held her breath as he fondled her. It was velvety compared to the satin smoothness of her breast. He brushed his finger back and forth until she bit her lower lip and shifted on his lap.

She moaned a sweet sound that he leaned up to capture in his mouth. She tipped her head to the side immediately allowing him access to her mouth. She held his shoulders and moved on him, centering herself over his erection.

She called his name as he brushed his cock against her humid center, straddling him so that just the tip of his erection was inside of her.

He scraped his fingernail over her nipple and she shivered in his arms. He pushed her back a little bit, so he could see her.

He held her still with a hand on the small of her back. He buried his other hand in her hair and arched her over his arm. He wanted Amelia more than he'd wanted a woman in a long time. He knew better than to let this mean anything more than one night with his ex. He wouldn't let this be about anything other than the physical.

She rocked her hips trying to take him deeper and he knew the time for teasing was at an end.

She leaned down and sucked his lower lip into her mouth, biting gently. He wanted to make her his, even as he knew no woman could ever be his. But in this moment, with the big Texas sky over them filled with stars, he could pretend.

He could claim Amelia as his…

Just for tonight.

She wasn't looking for anything permanent and Lord knew, he was a Delaney through and through, cursed to never keep a woman. He shoved that thought aside, giving her another inch of his cock, thrusting his hips up into her tight pussy. Her eyes were heavy-lidded as her hips moved frantically against him.

He sucked on the pulse beating in the side of her neck as he thrust all the way home. He knew he was leaving a mark with his mouth and that pleased him. He wanted her to remember this night later. To remember him when she woke the next morning. Part of his past was coming back to haunt him.

Her eyes widened with each inch he gave her. She

clutched at his hips as he started thrusting, holding him to her, eyes half-closed, and her head tipped back.

He leaned down and caught one of her nipples in his teeth, scraping very gently. She tightened around him, demanding more. He wanted to keep the pace slow, steady, but the pleasure between them was too much.

He felt her body tighten as he clutched her hips. Then she scraped her nails down his chest. His sac tightened, and his blood roared in his ears as he felt everything in his world center to this one woman.

He called her name as he came. She tightened around him and he looked up into her eyes as he kept thrusting. He saw her eyes widen and felt the minute contractions of her body around his as she was consumed by her own orgasm.

She wrapped her arms around his shoulders and kissed the underside of his chin.

He told himself they'd both gotten what they needed and as he wrapped his shirt around her and held her in the swing, he knew that was a lie. He hadn't gotten the distraction he'd been looking for. She'd taken away the sharpness of the pain of his sister's death, but she'd awakened a need in him for something he wasn't sure Amelia would deliver. Regardless of the curse, he wanted more than one night with her. Only he knew she wasn't someone who would stay. She always walked away.

Chapter Eight

HER BODY STARTED to cool down and her legs were getting stiff from straddling him, so she began to get up. She looked into his eyes, searching for something she couldn't define, but she didn't find it.

Did he regret this?

Amelia had hoped for closure after she and Cal had hooked up.

This was awkward.

Gingerly she lifted herself off his lap and then reached for her shirt, which luckily was big and fell to her hips.

He watched her and then stood up, turning his back, she assumed to do up his jeans, and she grabbed hers and shimmied into them.

"Um...I guess I should be going," she said.

He turned and looked over his shoulder at her. Again, his expression was inscrutable and she wanted to know what he was thinking. Or maybe it was a good thing she didn't know. He probably regretted this.

"Okay. I'll walk you to your car," he said.

She nodded. "I left my keys on the table in the hall."

He didn't say a word, just went to the front door and

opened it. He was back in a second with her keys, which he handed to her and then he walked by her side to the car. She wanted to run, get in the car, and then gun the engine as she drove away, leaving this moment in the dust.

How was it that something that had seemed so perfect just minutes earlier was now this?

That was *the Amelia touch.*

Her last boyfriend had mentioned that she seemed to find a way to sabotage every meaningful connection she ever had. All her romantic relationships and personal ones. And she had to admit, she was beginning to believe he was right. That had been another reason she'd come back to Last Stand. It was time to change things.

"Thanks for a nice evening," he said, holding open her door.

"You're welcome," she said, getting into the car. He shut the door and turned back toward the house. She started the car and drove away slowly, as if she hadn't realized just how screwed up she was at this moment.

She wanted to stay with Cal. She wanted to spend the night with him and hold him while he dealt with his grief for his sister. But instead, she'd done that thing she did.

She wanted to blame her mom. To say that if she hadn't found out the truth of her parentage when she'd been a teenager, she might be better at relationships. Her sisters agreed that she had a deal with always thinking that people were hiding something from her. Not in a paranoid or malicious way… Emma always added that, as if she wanted to make sure that Amelia didn't feel bad about her own failings.

As soon as she got to the main highway, she turned toward town but she wasn't concentrating on driving and pulled off to the side of the road.

What was she supposed to do?

She knew that sleeping with Cal while he was grieving was stupid. She was just as confused as she'd always been, now that she was back in Last Stand. And she hated the fact that despite thirty looming like a Dementor, she still felt like she was eighteen. When was she going to get mature and start making great decisions rather than ones that had long-term repercussions?

She liked Cal.

Dammit, she really liked him.

It wasn't that crazy-ass crush thing that she'd had back in high school. No, this was legit. But instead of being smart or sensible, she'd acted like her regular self. She put her head on the steering wheel of her car, banging it lightly.

She drove to her house. When she'd started making serious money from modeling, she'd purchased a few properties around the country, including this large ranch-style house. She was planning to remodel it now that she was home. Who knew how long she'd need to be here? She pulled into the driveway and noticed someone sitting on her front porch on one of the Cracker Barrel rockers that she'd purchased last year with her sisters on a road trip through Tennessee.

Her mom.

Amelia was definitely not in the mood to talk to her. She had been careful to never say anything that would upset her mom and maybe that was the reason that she hadn't been able to find closure.

The things she knew she wanted to say in her heart were mean and hurtful and she knew they would cut her mom, and that her dad—not her biological father—would never forgive her if she hurt her mom that way.

But she couldn't sit in the car without making her mom think something was wrong so she got out and walked toward the front porch.

"Hi, honey, I hope you don't mind but I couldn't sleep. My doctor suggested that walking might help. Anyway, I ended up here and thought I'd wait for you," she said.

This.

This was why she was here. Her mom was sick and not one doctor had been able to give them any prognosis that wasn't worrying. She had walked here but to be fair, Amelia's house was only a few blocks from her parents'. And the streets in Last Stand had nice sidewalks.

"Hi, Mom. Want to come inside?"

"Sure," she said.

She led the way into the kitchen nook and her mom took a seat on the padded bench under the window. Amelia got her a glass of lemonade, more to keep herself busy and to avoid having to sit down and talk.

"You okay?" Mom asked as Amelia handed her the drink and then sat down across from her.

"Yeah," she said. The lie felt thick and heavy on her tongue.

"You sure?"

She nodded. She couldn't make up any excuse her mom would believe. "I just needed some time. Being back home isn't what I expected."

"It never is," she said.

"When did you leave Last Stand?" she asked. Her mom had gone to college in Austin and lived at home. As far as Amelia knew, she'd never left. But then there were things about her mom she'd never known.

"When I found out I was pregnant with you."

"What?"

Her mom sighed and leaned down against the open window. "I was confused, and I didn't know what my mom would say. I loved Jasper, but he and I were just at the new part of the relationship, just falling in love and I didn't want…"

"Me?" she asked.

"No. Honey, never that," she said, scooting closer to Amelia on the bench and putting her arm around her. "I wanted you from the moment I learned I was pregnant."

She hugged Amelia close and Amelia hugged her back, resting her head on her mom's shoulder.

"But I made your life…complicated."

"You made my life," she said. "I was drifting before you. I got in my car at Doc McBride's after he told me and I just drove north. I didn't stop except for gas until I reached Oklahoma. I thought about just keeping going. But I was out of cash and back then, there weren't ATMs all over the place."

"So, you needed money," she said.

"Yes. I went into a bank to get them to cash a check and when they called the People's Bank of Last Stand...Jasper came on the line and asked to speak to me," her mom said.

"I bet that went well," she said.

"You know how Dad is. He was so calm. He said he'd already authorized the money, but he was worried about me and so were my parents. He said whatever I needed to do, he hoped I'd find some answers and that he was just going to wait for me to come back home. He said he loved me and that he wasn't going anywhere. That if it took me ten years of searching to realize I loved him too, fine. If it took forever—well, he hoped it didn't, but he was still going to love me. He said that's the way love works."

She blinked back the tears. Jasper wasn't a man of many words but he was wise. Hearing how much he loved her mom didn't surprise her at all, but it did touch her. She wanted a man to love her like that, but knew she had yet to figure out how to be a woman who would inspire that kind of devotion.

"Is that why you didn't go to Jax?"

"Oh, no," she said. "Um, are you sure you want to know about Jax?"

"Yes," she said. "Remember you promised me no more lies?"

"I do," she said. "But we're both going to need something stronger than lemonade for this story."

Amelia went to the fridge and pulled out a new bottle of white wine. She poured them both a glass and then because she couldn't drink without eating something or she got sick, she put a bowl of nuts and pretzels on the table as well.

Her mom took a healthy sip of the wine before Amelia even sat down.

"I tracked him down in LA after I'd talked to my parents. I didn't say anything to Jasper about being pregnant or anything like that. I just called Mom and Dad and then went to LA. I needed to know what Jax thought about you before I made any other decisions."

There was something tense and sad about her mom and a part of Amelia wished she hadn't asked for the truth. But she knew she needed to hear it. She needed to understand how her parents had thought that never telling her about Jax Williams was the right decision. They weren't horrible people, so she knew they'd done it to protect her.

"Anyway, I had to wait until the next morning for him to sober up. And I told him about you. He said he didn't want kids, that I was to see his attorney if I was after money, which I wasn't. And I told him that. After you were born he insisted I have a paternity test, which I did, then he asked me if I was going to keep you. I said yes, and he insisted that he wanted no part of your life. So we went to his attorney and signed some legal documents, which made you mine only. I called Jasper after that, telling him everything. He said that you weren't mine only, you were ours. He loved us both, and he wanted me to come home so we could start our family.

"And I did. We never thought about Jax again until he showed up at Memaw's house asking after me. Your dad and I were shocked that he wanted something from you. He'd signed away his rights."

Her heart was heavy and her mind racing with questions, thoughts and emotions that she wasn't ready to deal with. "But you couldn't turn him away, because of the baby."

"Exactly. We were stuck. There was no way an innocent child should pay the price for Jax's behavior back then. So we had you tested. Your dad said if you were a match, it was a sign that God wanted you to know."

Of course, he would. "Dad always believes that it's God's way, doesn't he?"

"He does. So, I took you to Houston and you know the rest. I wanted to tell you more, but you weren't interested in hearing anything else from us. I wanted to force you to listen—you know how I am. I hate letting anything go," she said, taking another sip of wine.

"Dad probably said I needed time." Amelia knew her father. He had likely thought that she'd reason out much of the story for herself. And if she'd been older, maybe she would have. But she had been sixteen and stubborn. "I was so hurt to think I wasn't really a Corbyn."

"You are a lot like me," her mom said. "But you are also a lot like your dad. Never doubt that you are every inch a Corbyn, honey. I know that you came home because of whatever is going on with me, but I hope you find some peace in Last Stand, the way I did when I got back."

She hugged her mom. It wasn't going to be easy. She still had questions and lingering hurts but she wanted peace and the happiness her mom had found. She didn't know if it would come with Cal or not, but she knew he was something she needed to put right as well.

BRADEN WAS WAITING in the den when he walked back into the house. His brother had two bottles of Lone Star in his hand as well as the baby monitor. This might be their new reality, he thought.

"I heard her leave and thought you might want some company. Damned sure I'm tired of pretending to work," Braden said.

"Pretending?" he asked, taking a bottle from his brother as he sat down in one of the big leather chairs that were situated in front of the floor-to-ceiling bookcases.

Braden sat down in the chair closest to him and took a long drag on his beer, tipping his head back.

"Yeah. For once work isn't the escape I need it to be. You know that Rose and her friends were going to man the Outlaw Tequila booth at the Bluebonnet Festival on Saturday and she left me all these notes with their names and numbers on them. Along with one that said, 'she's hot, you'll like her.'"

Braden's voice broke.

Cal reached over to squeeze his brother's shoulder as Braden looked away and took another swallow of the beer.

"Want me to take over organizing it?"

"Hell, no. It'll hurt you, too," Braden said.

"I'm the big brother," Cal added. He wasn't sure that really mattered but he was used to shouldering the burdens. Braden shouldn't have to deal with this. And besides, focusing on something might make it easier for him to stop thinking about Amelia.

He knew he shouldn't have hooked up with her tonight. Everything in his gut said the timing was wrong. He wasn't ready. She wasn't, either. But he hadn't been able to resist her and honestly, for a few brief moments, he'd forgotten about everything. That had been worth it.

"Do you ever think that Dad drank to ease the pain of missing Mom?" Braden said. "I always thought he was weak but tonight...I'm thinking drinking until I can't feel anything sounds like a damned good idea."

"Bray, that's not you. You'll just feel guilty in the morning and make yourself go to work with a hangover."

"Yeah, but at least I wouldn't be missing Rose tonight."

"I don't think it works that way," Cal said. "But if you want to try it, I'm happy to keep you company."

"I was hoping you and Amelia would...well it might be nice for you to have something to distract you tonight."

"Well, um, Amelia and I are like oil and water."

"I don't see that," Braden said. "You don't really fight."

"That's not what I meant. We just don't mix."

"Seemed like you two mix pretty well, but neither of you knows what to do with it," Braden said.

"Dude, did you see us on the porch?" he asked, a little freaked out.

"No! Was there something I shouldn't have seen? I just meant at dinner, she kept looking at you whenever she didn't think you were looking, and you did the same. I'm not a weirdo, Cal. When you guys went outside, I let you alone," he said.

"That was more me freaking out than any belief you would have watched us," Cal said.

"Want to talk about it?"

"No. Do I look like Dr. Phil?"

Braden just laughed and took another swallow of his beer. "I'm empty. Want another?"

"Yeah," he said. His brother had seemed more like his old self when he'd been laughing and despite everything, Cal felt a bit lighter.

He got up and grabbed them two more beers. Braden was still sitting where Cal had left him, staring sort of pensively at the floor. As much as he didn't want to talk about Amelia, maybe it was the thing to get Braden's mind off Rose.

"Thanks," Braden said as he handed him the bottle.

Before he could come up with anything to talk about, he got a text and glanced down at his phone as Braden's pinged.

It was from Finn.

The text was about the funeral. Finn was coming home, taking the week off from driving and he wanted them each to ask a friend to be a pallbearer.

"Well, hell. I guess we need to get focused on this," Cal said.

"Yeah. I'll ask Red," Braden said. "He offered to do anything we need, and he liked Rose."

"Yeah, he did. He always wanted siblings," Cal said. Red was like a brother to Braden and he'd hung out at the Delaney house a lot when they'd been growing up. They were still close.

He wasn't sure who he'd ask. Then realized that he could call his friend Wyatt Kelly. He and Wyatt had been friends for years. He wouldn't mind. After all, he'd already called and offered to help out in any way. And he was going to be in town on Saturday for the Bluebonnet Festival, to represent Kelly Boots. They had a new boot they'd designed for spring that had a bluebonnet on it.

"This week is going to be hard," Braden said. "The worst part is that life is still going to go on without her. I don't want to plan for her to permanently be gone."

"Me either, Bray. But there isn't anything else we can do."

"I wish that made it easier," Braden said.

"I think the fact that it doesn't is right. She was the heart of our family. And it's going to take a long time before we can heal from this."

They drank beers for another two hours before Braden went up to bed. Cal went to Lane's room and scooped up his sleeping nephew, who groused a bit and then settled on his chest and went back to sleep. Cal sat in the rocking chair in the nursery holding Lane for the rest of the night. But he couldn't get any closer to making peace with Rose's death or the fact that Amelia might leave again soon.

Chapter Nine

WEDNESDAY MORNING DAWNED as the perfect spring day. It was clear and sunny, with no chance of crazy winds or rain. Cal was glad of it. Though a rainy day would have suited his mood better as they prepared to bury Rose, he knew that he wanted her day to suit her and she'd always been sunny…well most of the time.

They'd all called friends to come and help out with various aspects of the funeral. Finn had brought his head mechanic, Zim, back with him from the road. His NASCAR sponsor had given him the next week off, which was probably a good thing, not just for Finn but for everyone. Of the three of them, Finn was having the hardest time containing his temper.

Braden had asked Red and Red had driven out to the Delaney property last night. They'd spent the night drinking and telling stories about Rose, which had been nice. Cal had invited Wyatt Kelly to come over, but he was getting ready for the summer boot release and hadn't been able to make it any earlier.

The doorbell rang, and Cal went to answer it. Wyatt had changed a lot since he'd gotten married. He was still a badass but there was something tame about him now. Cal had to admit there were times when he envied what his friend had found with Juliette. They were expecting a baby in about six months and domesticity suited him.

As soon as Wyatt could get away, he'd made his way to Last Stand. It was only about a twenty-minute drive and Cal didn't have words when he opened the door and saw his friend standing there the day of the funeral.

"I brought you this. Nick won it off a Scot who was at Booze's Place last weekend," Wyatt said holding out a bottle of Glenlivet.

Cal took the Scotch. Wyatt gave him a bro hug, patting him on the back. "I'm here for as long as you need me. Juliette told me not to come home if you needed a night of drinking or fighting. I think I'm getting on her nerves."

Cal smiled to himself. That sounded like Juliette. "Why are you getting on her nerves?"

"Well, you know she's pregnant. But we just found out we're having twins! And at her last doctor's visit, she found out she had hypertension. In fact, I should probably text her and make sure she's okay. I mean she was okay five minutes ago when I FaceTimed her to tell her I was here," Wyatt said.

"Dude, if you text her again, you should probably make plans to stay in the guest house indefinitely."

Wyatt laughed. "You're right. So, what do you need?"

"Nothing. We're going to the First Methodist church for the service and then we are going to bury her up on the hill by Mom and Dad."

"Damn, man, you've had too many funerals in your life," Wyatt said.

They heard a clip-clopping sound, and both turned to face the hallway where Lane came running toward them on his broomstick pony. His nephew hadn't comprehended what was going on today and Cal thought that was a good thing. Lane pulled his horse up short and looked up at Wyatt.

"Who you?"

"I'm Wyatt," Wyatt said, stooping down to Lane's level. "I'm here to help celebrate your mommy today. I brought you something."

Wyatt handed Lane a Kelly Boots box and his nephew set his broomstick horse aside and reached for the top of the box. Cal watched as Lane lifted the lid and pulled back the tissue the boots were wrapped in. He caught his breath as he saw the special design. Black boots with a pretty white climbing rose wrapping around a cowboy hat.

"Thanks," Lane said, sitting down to put the boots on. Cal had to look away as he felt tears burning his eyes.

He wasn't too proud to cry but this gesture from Wyatt meant more than Cal could take. "Made you and your brothers a pair each, too. They're in the car."

"Thanks, man. They're something else," Cal said, wiping his eyes.

"You need a minute? I've got this little cowboy," Wyatt said.

Cal nodded and walked down the hall into his den. He closed the door of the room and leaned his head back against the door. He was torn in two by Rose's death. There was a part of him that understood that it had been an accident, and then there was the darker part of his soul that was so afraid he'd driven her into carelessness by not being the big brother she'd needed him to be.

He heard the clip-clopping sound from Lane's broomstick horse again and knew his nephew was back to playing. Cal should get back out there, making sure his brothers were getting ready. But he couldn't make himself move.

There was a knock on the door and he scrubbed his hand over his eyes before opening it.

"Man, I can't do this," Finn said, coming inside. "Rose always helped me with my tie. But she's not here."

"I got this. I'll do it for you," Cal said. "How is it you don't know how to tie a tie?"

"I was always in a car and racing. We don't have to wear ties at all. And usually I keep it knotted and hanging in the closet but it got stuck on the hanger and…"

"You got pissed and ripped it off," Cal said.

"Yeah. I can't right now, Cal. Seriously, I don't know what's going on, but I have never felt this crazy inside before, not even when Mom died," Finn said.

"You got this. You just need some time to process it. Getting the news the way you did…I'm sorry I had to call."

"I would have kicked your ass if you hadn't. Zim said you told him before the race ended," Finn said, as Cal knotted his tie and then stepped back to straighten it.

"Yeah. I figured he would know when I should call you back," Cal said. Zim was like part of their family, and Cal knew Finn would need a friend once he got the news.

"He did. Shit, Cal. What are we going to do without our Rose?" Finn said.

"We're going to take one day at time," Cal said, focusing now on his brothers and not on his own grief. He clapped his hand on Finn's shoulder and led him out of the house to the big limo they'd rented for the day.

AMELIA HADN'T PLANNED to attend Rose Delaney's funeral. She wasn't sure that Cal would want to see her there but her parents had insisted. The First Methodist church, where the funeral would be held, was close to her parents' house and her mom had offered to hold the wake at their home after the service, since she thought the Delaney boys might not want to host it at their place. They'd taken her up on the offer.

Watching her mom and Memaw work together to get the Corbyn mansion ready for the wake made Amelia realize again how much she'd missed out by refusing to talk about the past. She still hadn't really gotten the closure she needed within herself. Once she'd heard her mom's story, there was no way she could be anything but sympathetic to what Lilly Corbyn had gone through. In her shoes, Amelia acknowledged she would have done the same thing.

"Come help me get the pans of food out of my van," Delilah said. Her sister had on her chef's whites but full makeup and her hair was done.

"Okay," Amelia said.

"Thanks," Delilah said as they started carrying the food into the house through the kitchen door. "What's up with you and Mom? You were staring at her when I walked in."

"Nothing. I mean, we talked the other night and I was just…wishing I hadn't been so stubborn and wasted so many years. Also, when I look at her sometimes it's hard to remember she's sick."

"I know what you mean. I asked Dad if he thought it might be all in her head and he about bit mine off. But she's in such good shape. She always has been. It's not right that she has something wrong with her," Delilah said.

"I know, Dee. I wish they could identify it so we'd be able to fight it. Or at least know what it was she was fighting."

"Me too," her sister said.

They put the last of the food on the counter and then were shooed out of the kitchen by the staff her mom had hired for the day. They had come over from Whiskey River and had served at her parents' parties before, according to Emma.

Amelia followed Delilah upstairs into her old bedroom where her sister was getting changed. She drifted into the playroom, which had been turned into a game room when they were teens and in the last few years had become a sitting room for overnight guests. She sat on the love seat that she had fond memories of squeezing onto with her sisters and both her parents for story time as a young girl.

She just stared down at the couch. For a long time, she'd

hated those memories of her childhood but now she felt fonder about them. She heard someone behind her and turned to see her dad standing in the doorway.

"You okay?"

"Yeah. Just thinking about how we used to all squeeze on here," she said.

"Those are some of my favorite memories," he said.

"Mine too," she admitted. "You know Mom and I talked the other night. I'd love to hear your side of things."

"What do you mean?" he asked, coming further into the room. He was dressed in a black three-piece suit and tie. His long leonine mane of hair had been slicked back and he was clean-shaven. She knew her dad thought some stubble was okay for the weekend but not the workweek and certainly not for weddings or funerals.

"Just...don't be offended please. But...did you resent me? Did you wish I wasn't a part of Mom?" she asked. She knew what her mother had said but that was her mom's perspective on Jasper. He might have felt differently and since she knew more of the story now, she wondered if he'd really felt the way that her mom had told her.

"Never. I never resented you," he said, coming further into the room. "I'm not going to pretend that it was easy to hear she was pregnant with another man's baby. But most of that was jealousy. I wanted her baby to be my baby. So, when Jax bowed out of her life, I was more than happy to take his place. I loved your mom from our very first date. And you were a part of that. You've been in our lives the entire time, Amelia. How could I not love you?"

She walked over to him and he hugged her close. "I didn't want to push you to find your way back because that would have done nothing but make you resentful."

"I know. I'm so stubborn."

"It's one of the worst Corbyn traits," he said.

"It is," she said feeling a little bit better that no matter what genetics might say, she was a Corbyn. A part of her had always known that, but she'd been afraid that her dad might not feel that way.

That was the most crippling part of fear, she thought. She hadn't asked her father how he felt before this moment because until she'd heard her mom's story, she was afraid that Jasper had been simply being nice to her all of her life. He was a generous man who always put others first, so it would have made sense. But hugging him close now, she knew that he was her father and that no one could take that away from her.

CAL WASN'T SURE how it happened but he, Wyatt and Braden were all playing poker with Memaw Corbyn after everyone else had cleared out of the Corbyn house. The funeral had been lovely or so he'd been told by everyone in town. He and his brothers had endured more sorrow than a body should have to, according to Mrs. Pullman, and the Ledgermans had offered their teenaged twins to babysit Lane.

It had been a long day, stretching his tolerance for people

to the limits. But somehow, sitting in the game room with Memaw Corbyn, drinking her homemade moonshine and watching her try to con Wyatt, was making up for it. Braden, who had downed two glasses of moonshine, was sort of swaying a bit in his chair. Jasper came in, saw Braden and steered him to one of the large leather couches in the sitting area of the room before taking his place at the table.

"Mom, are you playing nice?"

"I'm playing to win," Memaw Corbyn said. "Besides, this is Booze Kelly's son. He knows his way around a poker table."

"Mother."

"Don't be a stick in the mud, Jasper. These boys need to have some fun today," she said.

"Yes, ma'am. Deal me in, then," he said. "I'm not about to leave you to your own devices."

She chuckled but dealt him in. They were playing Texas Hold 'Em. Cal had a handful of crap each time and he'd suspected that Memaw was cheating but there was no way she'd be able to cobble together such bad hands that many times in a row. He folded and stood up, moving over to check on Braden who was gently snoring.

He heard someone behind him and noticed Jasper had left the table as well. "Figured I should leave the sharks to fight it out."

Cal laughed. "Yeah, they both seem to be playing at a different level."

"Indeed. You got a minute? I know today's not the day to talk business but I need to find out what you want to do about the loan that TJ initiated."

Damn. He'd forgotten about that. TJ's funeral tomorrow was being held over in Austin, since that's where his family was originally from, and Cal had promised Lancey Maverick they'd come and help her bury her brother. She didn't have much other family besides TJ and a couple of aunts who lived in Houston.

"Yeah, I guess so," Cal said.

"Let's go into my office," he said leading the way.

Cal noticed that Amelia was sitting near Finn and Zim, talking to them. She glanced up when he walked by and then blushed and looked away. The last time he'd seen her, she'd been driving away from him, hell-bent for leather.

Damn, his life was a mess. The only woman who he couldn't forget kept leaving him. That had to mean something totally messed up. Amelia had shaped the way he looked at relationships. He wasn't blaming her. In fact, she'd sort of reinforced what he already believed about his own cursed ancestry. Even Rose couldn't escape it.

"You okay, son?"

"Yes, sir. What do you need to know about the loan?"

"Lancey Maverick called the bank the other day. She wanted to find out if her brother had finished signing the paperwork. She has put in for an early release from the Marines and she thought she'd take over the mortgage on the shop. I told her I needed to check with his partner first," Jasper said. "Do you want a drink?"

After the moonshine, he didn't think he should have anything else. Drinking took the edge off his grief for a little while but then it turned his thoughts dark. He knew it was time to stop. "Coffee would be great."

"I'd like one, too," he said. "I never got to show you the plans that TJ had submitted for the loan. They're in this folder. Why don't you take a look while I get the coffee?"

Cal took the folder from Jasper and sat down on one of the armed wing chairs and opened it up. The first thing that struck him was that TJ had taken his time with the plans. His handwriting was neat and he addressed every concern. In one section, he was brutally honest, mentioning that he wanted Cal to be his partner so that if he screwed up, Rose and Lane would be protected.

Damn.

He shook his head. This was something that he couldn't deal with today. Or ever. He wanted to just leave Last Stand and keep driving until he was in a big city somewhere, where no one knew him and he wouldn't have to face this.

But that wasn't realistic. He had to act like the eldest Delaney. He needed to make sure that TJ's dream lived for Lane. Lane would know that his father had been determined to make sure he had a future.

By the time Jasper came back, he had a better idea of the man that TJ had slowly been becoming. Some of the stuff in his five-year plan was taken from a textbook from a business class that he was taking in college. Cal only knew that because TJ put it in his notes.

For the first time, he realized what Rose had seen in her young man. Why hadn't he been able to see it before it was too late? Maybe if he'd been more accepting…?

But there was no going back. He just had to make sure that Lane was given all the love and support he would have had from TJ and Rose. And he'd also make sure Lane knew the kind of parents he'd had.

He thought about Amelia then and her parental situation. It made it easier for him to understand the way she'd left him but the impact of those actions still lingered. Understanding it didn't really mean a damned thing. He needed to figure out how to move past her. Unfortunately, she'd always been the only woman he'd ever really wanted.

Chapter Ten

THE SATURDAY OF the Bluebonnet Festival dawned bright and sunny. Amelia hadn't seen Cal all week. She and her family had attended the funeral for Rose but he and his brothers were with their friends afterward and she had the feeling that drinking and talking was what he needed so she'd left him alone.

Emma was working a booth for the Friends of the Library and had invited her—well, more like told her—to work a shift. She noticed a line around the Outlaw Tequila booth and saw they had set up a huge OUTLAW TEQUILA WANTED poster and had a photographer taking souvenir pictures. The line was long, and she couldn't help but notice a lot of kids were in the line with their parents. Braden and Cal were working the booth, talking to patrons as she walked by, and a woman she didn't recognize handed her an Outlaw Tequila bandana, which she took but kept on walking.

She tied it around her neck like a kerchief as she took her spot in the Friends of the Library booth. The house she'd purchased had been sold as an estate sale and she'd found tons of boxes of books in the attic. She'd sorted through five of them so far and had donated the ones she didn't want to keep in her personal collection.

"Hiya," Emma said as she finished up a sale. "I thought you were going to ignore my text."

"Never. I wasn't doing anything except trying to stay away from the funnel cakes. They are my weakness."

"You could have one," Emma said gently. "You're not modeling anymore. I mean…well, you know what I mean."

"I could, but it's like a gateway food. I'll start with a funnel cake and the next thing you know, I'm eating a corn dog, then barbecue… It just won't end," she said. She'd left Last Stand to model to escape the past and because she wanted more than this small town had to offer. And she had enjoyed modeling and traveling the country. Now that she was back home, she had expected to feel the pull of New York. But instead, she was starting to…well, like it here.

"I'm going to have one later and you can have a bite— just one—of mine," Emma said with a wink.

"Deal," she said.

"What else do you miss that you had to give up?" Emma asked.

"You and Delilah. Kolaches. Memaw," she said, even though an image of Cal Delaney popped into her head. His wide muscled shoulders, icy-gray eyes and chiseled jaw. The way he'd looked when she'd been straddling him on his front porch. A jolt of awareness went through her and she turned away from her sister, looking down at the pile of books nearest her. The cover showed a shirtless man wearing a pair of low-slung jeans with washboard abs… Cal had abs like that. He could probably—

"Didn't you miss anyone else?" Emma persisted.

"Who could compete with you, Ems?" she asked.

"Of course, you did. I meant—okay I stink at this. Delilah told me that one of her kitchen workers saw you leaving the Delaney ranch late on Monday night…so…"

"So?" she asked, stalling for time. She wasn't ready to talk about Cal but then again, she hadn't come to any great conclusions on her own.

"Are you getting back with Cal?" she asked.

She glanced up from the books, looking around the booth, which was empty at the moment, and then turned back to her sister. "I don't know. My timing stinks as usual, with Rose and everything. But I like him."

"Yay. I was hoping you'd say that. What about joining the community committee? Then you can see Cal and help out in town. Dad is really keen to retire in a few years, but he won't unless he feels like we Corbyns are doing our part."

"But—"

"Don't you dare say what I think you're about to say," Emma said. "That's nonsense."

"I wasn't going to say that," she said, laughing. Her sisters were both fierce in their defense of her and how they always made sure to remind her she was a Corbyn too.

"What were you going to say?"

"I don't want Cal to think I'm stalking him," Amelia said. "I'm trying to give him space and see what happens."

"Give him space?" Emma asked. "Men aren't like that, honey. How many times have Mom and Memaw both said you have to show them what they want?"

"A lot. But I'm not sure what worked for them will work for us. Plus...I can't talk about this now, but stuff happened...and then I was me and made it awkward. What's the drill here?"

"Are you kidding me? You can't drop that and then be all how do I do this job? I want to know more."

"I'll tell you later. I don't want to talk about it here."

"Fair enough. But I'm not letting you out of it," she said.

"I need some sensible advice," Amelia said. "Now what do I do?"

"Just ring up the sales and put the money in the cash box. Pretty straightforward. I'm going to be working with you for most of your shift."

"Good, we haven't had much time to catch up. I had no idea you were so busy," she said. "Honestly, whenever I thought about your job, I pictured you sitting behind a desk, reading and then shushing people who are too noisy."

Her sister shook her head. "That's so insulting. It'd be like me saying when I thought of you modeling, I pictured drinking water and making bitchy faces."

"Uh, yeah, that's what I did. It's called living the dream," Amelia said, sticking her tongue out at her sister.

"I know it's more than that."

"I know your job is too. It's just when I think of you, you're always tucked away and reading."

"Nothing wrong with that," Joey said, stepping into the booth. She was another librarian who worked with Emma.

"I agree," Amelia said. Realizing she was surrounded by serious bookworms, she decided to stop teasing her sister.

The hours flew by as she worked her shift with Emma and Joey.

"Hello, ladies. I hope I'm not too late." It was the familiar rumble of Cal's voice.

"Perfect timing. Joey and I have to run over to the Fuhrmann statue for story time with the kids," Emma said, taking Joey's arm and leading her away with a wave over her shoulder at Amelia.

Her sister was meddling and Amelia couldn't say she minded. At least this way, she'd have something to talk about that wasn't the way she'd left.

"How've you been?" he asked.

"Okay. I'm sorry for the way I took off the other night," she blurted out. Yeah, good thing she didn't have to talk about that, but she'd never been good at doing what she should.

⁂

CAL COULDN'T HELP but laugh at the way she'd said that. He just shook his head. "Honestly, don't sweat it. This has been one of the oddest weeks of my life."

It had been, but he didn't want to go into that. Today, he was doing what he'd been trying to master for most of the week. Faking it. Just smiling when he could, talking to friends and neighbors who knew him and had learned that his sister was gone.

When Emma's text had come through a few minutes ago, it had been a godsend. He'd noticed August Wolf walking toward him and had decided he wasn't ready to talk to him. His attorneys had been taking care of paying for the repairs to August's storefront wine shop since Rose had clearly been responsible for the accident. He hadn't really had a chance to get to know August, and today, he simply hadn't been up to a casual chat. So he'd texted Emma that he'd come right over.

But maybe this hadn't been his best idea. Talking to Amelia wasn't a hardship. She'd been on his mind a lot this week and frankly, when he'd been close to wigging out and losing his sanity, he'd remembered her in his arms on the porch swing. It had sort of been his touchstone to sanity. It gave him something to think about, but not worry about.

He hadn't been the one to walk away, so he had no guilt with their encounter as he sometimes had back in his playing days. But that was a long time ago and he scarcely recognized the man he'd been.

"I bet it has. I wasn't sure what you needed so I decided to give you some space. But I felt like such a weasel after I left you that night. I just didn't know what to say. Sometimes, I'm one big hot mess...okay not sometimes. I mean Delilah would say—"

He put his finger over her lips. She was talking too much, something he'd noticed she did when she was nervous.

"It's okay. Thank you for coming to her service and wake."

"You're welcome," she said and then hugged him. He pulled her closer than he should because he could tell she'd meant the embrace to be a friendly one, but he needed more. Everyone he'd spoken to had been so gracious that it was starting to leave him a little bit on edge. Every once in a while, it became too much and he made use of the punching bag he had in his office, hitting it until his knuckles hurt and the feeling passed.

"Hey, do you want to spend some time together later? I have to head back to the Outlaw Tequila booth, but maybe after that?" he asked.

She stepped back as a couple with two kids entered the Friends of the Library booth and greeted them. More people followed and he helped them before they were alone again.

"I'd like that," she said. "I hear there's a band playing live music somewhere in the park. It might be nice to see if your dance skills have improved since homecoming junior year."

"Don't get your hopes up," he said. "I'm pretty much the master of the sway and of course, I can do the Cotton Eye Joe."

"Of course," she said. For some reason, Last Stand High School's PE program had included a two-week block of country western dancing when they'd been in tenth grade. "Me too. I have to be honest—I never used those skills in New York."

"Mrs. Jones promised wherever life took us, we'd appreciate knowing the dance moves. For myself, I did use them once—when our team made the playoffs. For some reason, we did a very bizarre version of it as a promo for our fans."

She shook her head. "How did I not know about this? Is it on the web?"

"God, I hope not," he said, but laughed at the memory. Rose had thought it was the funniest thing ever and had made a gif of him doing it. He smiled at the memory. The pain was still there, but this time, didn't hurt as much as it had. Which made him feel sort of guilty and sad. But before the feeling could take root, Amelia rubbed his back.

She knew.

She got that he was dealing with each moment and balancing between what was happening and what had happened.

"How?" he asked.

"In no way did my problems with my family match your loss. But when I found out everything from my parents, it was the same. I would have this happy memory and then suddenly recall I wasn't who I thought I was."

There was so much more to this woman than he'd realized, and he couldn't help himself as he leaned down and kissed her. She wrapped her arms around his waist and held him close.

He heard the sound of clapping, and he lifted his head to meet Finn's gaze.

"The library is a lot friendlier than I remember."

He shot his brother the bird and ignored him. "Are you here to work the next shift?"

"Hell, no. Braden wanted me to stop by and tell you that you don't have to come back and work the booth. Javier and his team from Tequila are there. They are doing a demonstration and they'll cover your shift."

"Great so I'm free. Want to spend the afternoon with

me?" he asked.

As soon as the workers arrived for the next shift, he took Amelia's hand in his and led her away from the booth toward the food section. He wasn't going to think about anything except this day and this moment. And for now, that would be enough.

⚜

NOTHING HAD GONE according to her plan since she'd come back to Last Stand and she was beginning to think that was a good thing. When they wandered to the section that had all of the food booths set up, she realized it was going to be harder than she thought to resist the funnel cakes, and other junk food. Especially since Cal hadn't met anything fried he didn't like.

"Have a bite of this. Oh, my God, you'll love it," he said, holding out a fried Snickers bar.

She leaned in and his fingers brushed her chin as he held the bar close enough for her to take a bite. She held a napkin under her chin as she did so and then closed her eyes when the explosion of fried, sweet goodness hit her mouth.

"That is good," she said, swallowing.

"Want another bite?" he asked, wriggling his eyebrows at her.

"No. You have it," she said. He polished it off before spotting another food booth that he wanted to stop in.

She knew that she was going to have to run at least five miles tomorrow but seeing Cal enjoy himself was totally worth it. She stopped mentally tracking the calories of each bite and decided to join him instead.

He was ordering a smoked barbecue plate when she walked over to him with two mugs of local craft ale. "Make it two."

"Finally getting hungry?" he asked, as he paid for the plates, taking them from one of the local high school athletes whose club was sponsoring the booth.

"Yes," she said leading the way to a bunch of tables that were set up under a shade tent. They found a seat on the edge where they could hear the live rock 'n' roll music playing.

She took a long sip of her beer and closed her eyes for a second as she felt an odd sense of déjà vu. It had been so long since she'd been home, she'd forgotten what it felt like to be a part of something. But suddenly that feeling was back. And she relished it.

She felt justified in staying away for so long but after talking to her mom, she'd realized that her parents were just people. They were doing the best they could, the same as she was. The revelation had been a long time coming.

"What are you thinking about?"

"My mom."

"How's that going? After what you told me, I think I'd have a hard time forgiving too," he said.

"After our night together, I went home and found Mom there. She sometimes can't sleep, so she'd walked over to my place," Amelia said. "She talked to me about the past and it was not what I had expected at all."

"Was it good?" he asked.

"Yes, it was. I mean, there is still a teenager in me who's holding on to a few things, but as a woman, I get the choices she made. It wasn't easy for her or my dad," Amelia said. "I probably sound like a brat saying that."

"Not at all. I think it would be hard for anyone to deal with that. No matter your age," he admitted. "I was really hard on Rose when she told me she was pregnant. Now, I wonder what the point was. Should I have just let her and TJ live together? Maybe I was—"

"Stop," she said, putting her hand over his. "Looking back, it's always easy to see what you should have done. That's not productive at all."

"Rose made choices too. Part of it was influenced by you but from what I remember of her as a girl and from what you said, she was as strong-willed as the rest of you Delaneys. There wasn't a thing you could have done to change her mind once she made it up," Amelia said.

"That's true. But maybe if I'd done something different... It's those kinds of thoughts I've been trying to avoid. But I just can't."

"I know," she said. Her heart ached for the pain in his voice. "One thing I know for certain is that everything you did was out of love. I'm pretty sure she knew that too."

"I hope so. I yelled at her the morning she left. No one knows that but me and Rose, since everyone else was gone. We had a fight about TJ. I thought he'd flaked out again and she screamed at me to butt out of their lives. Then later in the day, I found out that TJ was trying to get a loan from the bank to open his own business," Cal said, putting his fork down next to his plate.

He didn't say anything else, but he didn't need to. She saw the regret and the castigation he was putting himself through. "What did you do? Try to stop the loan?"

He shook his head. "Of course not. I wouldn't do that."

"See, you weren't as bad as you think you were. Rose and TJ were young. Heck, I know better than anyone that at that age, you want the world to think you have your shit together. But she was probably just winging it, hoping it all worked out. The fact that you didn't have a picture-perfect last moment is okay too, because it means that your relationship was real. You fought, you loved, you had each other's backs and you probably teased the heck out of each other. Remember that you were her big brother, Cal. She loved you."

Chapter Eleven

"WHERE'S LANE TODAY?" she asked as they walked through the craft area a little later that afternoon.

"We divided the day into shifts. Finn had him for breakfast. Those two both love sugary cereal so they start the day with that. Then Finn races him around the dirt track on the back of the property," Cal said.

"That sounds dangerous," she said. "Is it safe for Lane?"

Cal pushed his plate away. "Yeah. Finn rigged up one of those kiddie car engines in a go-cart so it doesn't move fast and the weight is distributed on the frame so it won't flip. He had his head mechanic Zim help him. They were both so proud when they gave it to Lane last Christmas."

She smiled at that. She could totally see Cal's car-crazy, speed-loving brother wanting to get his nephew into a vehicle. Even if his nephew was only a toddler. "When is your shift?"

"In about twenty minutes. I'm taking him to the rides. Wanna come?" he asked wriggling his eyebrows at her. "I promise you lots of junk food and some rides that won't make the food come back up."

She did want to come with him. But was it the best idea?

She probably shouldn't be encouraging anything that would deepen the relationship between them. She was in Last Stand for now, because her mom needed her. But that didn't mean she'd be staying for good. Besides, she was a mess. Look at her crazy behavior when they'd slept together.

He had a look on his face that she hadn't seen since before Rose's accident and she didn't want him to lose it. She didn't want to think about why his happiness meant so much to her, but she knew that it did and she wasn't going to let him down. Or herself. She might not have come home looking for closure to the past but the truth was, she'd never forgotten Cal. Seeing him again had reminded her of how much she had always cared about him.

"I'd love to. Do we have to go back to the Outlaw Tequila booth to get him?"

"No. I think Bray took him to the storytelling that Emma was hosting. Let me text him and find out where he is," Cal said.

He took his phone out for the first time since he'd been with her. It was something she really appreciated since most of her dates before coming back to Last Stand always had their phone in their hand, scrolling through their social media feeds, more engaged with the device than her. But Cal was different.

He always had been and that was why she liked him. She realized that she was kidding herself if she thought she was doing anything this afternoon for Cal. She was doing it for herself. Ever since she was sixteen, she'd felt that there was something broken and wrong with her, that she was someone unwanted and unlovable. More than anything, she had wanted to be worthy of someone's love. To belong.

Well, shit.

She hadn't expected to get that deep while she was sitting here watching Cal. But there it was. Unexpected, but true. She'd lost her place when she'd learned her real parents had no relationship and her biological father hadn't wanted her. She knew that Jasper loved her, and she knew he wished she was his true daughter.

"He's going to come and meet us," Cal said. Then his brow furrowed as he took in her face. "You okay?"

"Yeah. I'm fine. I just had a...moment," she said at last. She had no way of explaining her sudden revelation, and honestly, she didn't want to talk about it. She forced a smile. "I am looking forward to the rides. When we were little, we always got one book of tickets each. So we had to be choosy about which ones we rode."

"Yeah, when Mom was alive, she used to give us each a book but after that...well, I don't think Dad even knew anything was going on if it didn't happen at the ranch."

She remembered Cal's dad as a very distant figure. He was almost always absent when she was out at his house. She had Jasper and was upset because he wasn't her real dad, but compared to Cal's situation, hers wasn't that bad. At least she had been loved and she had always known that her parents would be there for her. Even when she was acting like a brat.

"I'm sorry."

"Don't be. Once I started working, I made sure the boys

and Rose always had tickets and money."

"Unca!"

Amelia turned as Braden walked up with Lane. They were both dressed in jeans and CARS T-shirts and Lane was talking animatedly to Cal who had stooped down to be on his nephew's level. The words weren't clear enough for Amelia to follow but Cal seemed to understand and nodded a lot.

Braden looked over at her. "He got a new belt with his name on it at the craft fair."

"Oh, I heard belt, but that was it," she said.

"Yeah, we live with him all the time so we understand him. You pick it up really quickly."

She nodded. She wondered if Braden thought she'd be around a lot. "I bet. How was the craft fair?"

"The usual mix of exotic and quality. I thought about getting your grandmother a wooden statue of a dog, but remembered she has all those taxidermied ones. How was the food?"

She shook her head. Memaw was famous for her "pets." "I only tried the fried Snickers bar—delicious and the brisket also very good. Your brother ate everything else, I think."

Cal stood up, holding Lane's hand. "It was all good. I'll have to work out and run tomorrow but it was totally worth it. Are you hungry?"

He glanced down at Lane who nodded. "Corn dog?"

"Yes," Lane replied.

"Bray, you want to hang with us and grab something to eat?" Cal asked.

"I can't. I have to get back to the booth," Braden said. "I told Finn I'd take his shift. Javier and his team are doing the demonstration but I still like for one of us to be there."

"What's he doing?"

"More like who," Braden said with a laugh, walking away.

Cal slipped his free hand in hers and the three of them got Lane a corn dog, then walked toward the midway. Amelia stopped worrying about the future and just let herself enjoy this happy moment with Cal and his nephew.

꙰

CAL WATCHED LANE and Amelia sitting on the grass to the side of one of the music tents. His nephew had ridden every ride in the kiddie section, then shared his cotton candy with them before getting sleepy.

"Are you sure you don't mind?" he asked.

"I'm positive. Go on. I'm happy to sit here and watch him sleep and listen to the music. Plus if I keep walking around with you, I'm going to gain another ten pounds."

"You look good, darlin'. You don't need to worry about that," he said.

"You say that now, but I have no willpower. I'm already thinking about next week's dinners and they are all cotton candy and corn dogs."

He sat down next to her on the blanket, leaning close to steal a kiss. Something about Amelia made him feel a little bit lighter. Life hadn't been that hard—no way was he going to complain about the blessed life he had been living since college—but there were times when he felt the weight of taking care of family. But with her, the weight seemed a little less.

She turned her head, leaning it on his shoulder and looking down at Lane who was curled up next to them on the blanket. "I wish this was real."

Her words were spoken softly, but he heard them. "What do you mean?"

She sat up a bit so she could make eye contact with him. "Just that tomorrow, it will be back to normal. I'll still be a mess and trying to figure things out. But right now, sitting on this blanket with you, everything sort of feels okay."

"It is okay. You are okay," he said.

"I am?"

"I think so," he said. "Don't think about it too much. One thing I learned when I went to college was that everyone is dealing with something. When I was younger, it had seemed like everyone else's families were perfect and mine was the only one that was so messed up. Even your life seemed cushy, but you were dealing with stuff then and now. Everyone is doing that."

She gave him that sweet smile that shouldn't have turned him on but did. "How'd you get to be so smart?"

"I've made a lot of mistakes. Maybe I'm not smart—it might just be a food coma starting, considering everything I ate."

She laughed like he'd wanted her to. "You did eat a lot."

He had been planning to go home and do some work on

the ranch because that was what was expected of him, but he decided that for today, he'd done enough. He needed this break with Amelia and Lane. This moment was different than he'd expected it to be.

His phone pinged but he wasn't in the mood to deal with it. His brothers were all fine and there wasn't anyone he wanted to be with more than Amelia. "Want to dance?"

"Sure," she said. "Right here?"

"Why not?" he asked.

"Why not, indeed," she said, standing up. The grass was soft and thick and she'd taken off her wedge sandals. She wiggled her toes in the grass as he stood up next to her, pulling her into his arms.

The band was pretty good; their lead singer had a raspy voice that lent itself to many rock songs. They danced to classic songs and when they covered the 3 Doors Down ballad 'Here Without You,' they both stopped. "Remember eighth grade?"

"Yes. This was the slow song at every dance. And Principal McMillan would only allow that one."

He pulled her into his arms. Back then, he'd been a sort of sway-from-side-to-side guy and was always trying to let his hands drift down to his date's hips, but now, he didn't have to worry about the chaperones yelling at them. He put his hands on Amelia's hips and she wrapped her arms around his shoulders and sang under her breath as he held her closer than he probably should.

But after everything that had happened in the last week, he realized that all his rules for living were out the window.

There was no should or shouldn't. There was only what was right in the moment. And this was definitely right.

Her curves pressed against him and she smelled of sunshine and fair food as he rested his cheek on top of her head and closed his eyes. He had never felt this content with any other woman. Only Amelia Corbyn. The one woman who had sort of screwed up all his relationships.

It made no sense. He should be backing away from her but instead, he just wanted to stay by her side. Keep her by his side. His mind warned him that trusting this moment was a bad idea, but his gut urged him to pull her closer and forget about that. She tipped her head back and their eyes met. He lowered his head, kissing her as they danced to the music. The song ended but he still held her. Looking into her sky-blue eyes, he felt something shift inside of him. Lust, of course, but something else—something that scared him. Something emotional that he didn't trust.

The band said they were going to crank it up a notch and he heard the beginning guitar riff from 'Good Times All Night,' which was one of his favorite songs from Jax Williams. He glanced over at Amelia. Jax was her dad…what did that mean to her?

"I hate this song," she said.

"Why?"

"I think because I imagine that he's singing about the night I was conceived," she said. "I used to like him until I found out."

He nodded. *This was her reality.* He wondered if she'd ever be able to really trust a man after what Jax had done to her.

AMELIA FELT SORT of cheap and dirty when she listened to this song. She really didn't want Cal to see her that way. It was one of the few things she hadn't been able to really step away from, where Jax was concerned. He was a stranger to her. She'd only met him at the hospital for a brief moment. He'd wanted to conduct everything through his attorney but Amelia had insisted he at least meet her before she allowed them to take her bone marrow.

The procedure was painful but once she'd seen that tiny baby, her half brother, she knew there was no way she could deny him the chance to be healthy. He'd been so tiny, much like little Lane she thought, glancing down at the sleeping child. And innocent.

Jax hadn't said more than two words to her and her mom had wrapped her arms around Amelia after Jax had left. But she'd been so hurt by the entire thing.

"Want to talk about it?"

"I wouldn't even know where to start. He's a stranger to me, Cal. I can't say he was mean to me or abused me, but I don't know him at all. And he likes it like that. You know I've never even met my half brother."

"I'm sorry. Do you want to?"

"No. I mean I don't think so. I heard Jax left them, too. He's back to his old ways. Good times all the time."

CAL DIDN'T KNOW how to help her with this. He hugged her close, rubbing his hands up and down her back. "Some men just don't know how to love."

"You think so? How hard can it be just to let someone care for you?" she said.

"It's not that part," he explained because he was pretty sure his father had experienced something similar to this. "It's that he might not feel worthy."

She bit her lower lip, crossing her arms around her waist and holding herself. For the first time since she'd come home, he had an idea he was seeing the real reason she'd run away to New York. He had to wonder if he'd have done anything differently.

Hell, he hadn't. He'd left his family behind for college and really relished his new team family. When he was there, no one knew anything except he had a wicked arm and could hit just about any receiver even in thick coverage. It was what he'd needed. A chance to just forget about the mess that he had left back here in Last Stand.

"Do you?" she asked. "Is that why you are always trying to be in control?"

Her comments were a little too spot-on for comfort, but they weren't going to talk about him. This was her issue. She was the one who needed him right now. And he had big shoulders.

"I'm not talking about me," he said at last. He wasn't sure of the right thing to say to make this better for her. But he knew that if he kept talking, she might stop worrying over whatever was going around in her mind. She'd done that for him on the porch swing, given him something other than his own pain and guilt to dwell on. And he'd really like to be able to help her out now.

"I think it can happen to a man or a woman. Just depends on the events of their life. My dad didn't always feel that way but after Mom died, he was never the same. I really don't know Jax's story. I mean, I used to like a few of his songs but who knows what devil is driving him."

"I don't know, either. One time I started to google him but then I stopped. What was the point, right? It was just a lose-lose situation for me," she said.

"How do you mean?" he asked.

She looked away from him, turning her head toward the tent where the band was playing, a pensive look on her face. "Maybe I'd find a man I wanted to know and regret that I didn't and that would make me wonder why he never wanted me. What was wrong with me?"

"Darlin', nothing is wrong with you," he said briefly, wondering if he should make a joke and lighten the mood. But he had the feeling she hadn't had a chance to ever talk about this and he didn't want to stop her.

"It's not rational to think that, is it? But there is a part of me that can't help it. And this makes me feel petty and spiteful. But I don't want to understand him, Cal. I need to hate him. It's the only thing that keeps me from really losing it."

"Let's get out of here," Cal said. "Unless you want to be

alone?"

"I'd like to go somewhere with you," she admitted.

"How about the river?" he suggested.

She nodded. Delilah's restaurant, Dragonfly, was on the river, built on platforms with stilts to protect against flooding. But the rains hadn't started yet and the river was low so it would be nice to go and sit by its banks. Actually, even sitting in a traffic jam would be preferable to listening to this cover of Jax Williams's music and thinking.

Cal carefully picked up his nephew and the drowsing child settled easily on his shoulder. Amelia folded up the quilt that she'd purchased at one of the vendors earlier. She followed him to his truck and he drove the few blocks to the river parking in Red's Outdoor Outfitters' parking lot. They got out of the truck and he carried Lane in his arms down to the river.

"When I left Last Stand, I swore I'd never come back or allow anyone to get close to me again," she said. "That's why I never contacted you. I know you didn't ask, but it wasn't you. It was me trying to be strong and prove that I didn't need you. But you know what? There were times when I really did."

Chapter Twelve

I T WAS GOOD Friday night. Almost two weeks had passed since she'd slept with Cal, one week since the Bluebonnet Festival. Delilah had a rare night off. She and her sisters had decided to have a girls' night out. It had been a long time since they'd hung out without one of them having to rush off to work and Amelia had to admit, she was really looking forward to it.

They were meeting at Emma's place because she lived closest to the Last Stand Saloon. She walked into Emma's house through the kitchen door and heard Ariana Grande's 'God Is A Woman' blasting, and saw her sister dancing around the kitchen counter while mixing up martinis.

"Hiya, Ems."

"Hey!" Emma said, with a big smile. "I got off early so I'm making some of Memaw's secret moonshine and lavender cocktails."

"Oh, it's going to be one of those nights," Amelia said with a laugh. She could use a night out like this. She'd been avoiding Cal because she felt like she'd been too raw with him. And in all honesty, he didn't need her messy life on top of everything that was going on with him. She had to decide if she was staying in Last Stand and she couldn't do it for Cal. She had to come back because she wanted to live here, wanted this life. And frankly, she wasn't ready to risk that. Even though she knew that she was never going to love another man the way she did Cal.

"I know you don't mind," Emma said. "I just finished reading a book that was so...so me. The protagonist is always waiting for something to happen in her life and misses the fact that there are events and situations all around her. And people..."

"You okay?" Amelia asked her sister.

"Yeah. Just feeling not...me lately. I'm glad we are doing this," Emma said. "I want to hear about your thing with Cal, too. You two seemed to really be getting along at the Bluebonnet Festival."

"I think we were too, but we'll see."

"Are you two talking without me?" Delilah said as she came into the kitchen. "You always do that."

"We haven't said anything important except to establish it's a moonshine and lavender kind of night," she said.

"Perfect. I need it. I have a new chef at the Dragonfly who is getting on my last nerve. It's like he doesn't realize what I hired him for."

"You'll whip him into shape," Amelia said.

"I certainly will," she said taking a highball glass from Emma and handing it to Amelia first.

When they all had a glass, Amelia lifted hers toward her sisters. "To the bond of sisterhood and the friendship that never ends."

They clinked their glasses and took a sip. Emma had mixed them strong, but they went down smoothly. "Yum. So, Ems is feeling restless, you have a new chef who's annoying and I slept with Cal and then left in the most awkward way possible."

Delilah blinked at her, then took another sip of her drink. "I think we're going to need a few more of these to get through all of that. Also, Mom saw her doctor today and it's not good news."

"Well, hell," Emma said. "She was supposed to text me."

"Dad told me when I stopped by to drop off some blackberry cobbler I made earlier," Delilah said. "Guess we should start with Mom."

Amelia felt that cocktail of guilt and fear and anger that her mom always stirred in her. She walked into the family room and sat down on one of the large padded fabric recliners, taking a sip of her drink while her sisters followed her into the room. "Okay, Dee, what do you know?"

"She's not showing any improvement and they still can't commit to a diagnosis. Dad says she can't sleep and sometimes, she feels like the walls are closing in on her. So the doctor has recommended she exercise more. Dad wants us to have a family meeting tomorrow morning. He was going to text y'all but I said I'd tell you. I'll stop at Kolaches and get breakfast. We're meeting at Memaw's because Dad wants Mom to walk over there," Delilah said.

This didn't sound good. It sounded scary. Amelia was afraid for her mom. She felt her hands shaking and it seemed to her that maybe moving back home permanently was what she needed to do so she could be surrounded by people she cared about instead of a career that had lost its glamour. "Did they say anything in particular? Name any condition that Emma can research and I can ask my doctor friends in New York about?"

"No. Her symptoms aren't exact enough for the doctor to feel confident…"

"You said that," Emma said.

"I know. It sort of pisses me off. If someone ordered, say, a chicken fried pork chop at the Dragonfly and I gave them meat loaf, they'd be angry. It's the same thing. They are trained—they should know something," Delilah said.

"I agree," Amelia said. "This is different, and you know it. My office is near the medical center. I'll stop by on Monday and see if we can find out anything else. Maybe find another place to look for answers."

"Thanks," Emma and Delilah said at the same time.

"It's good to have you home," Emma said. "Between the three of us, we will be able to take good care of Mom."

Her sisters both looked at her and she realized they expected her to say she couldn't.

"Yes, we will," Amelia said. "Mom and I talked the other day. We are working through some things."

"Good, it's about time," Emma said. "Now, tell us about Cal."

She groaned. "Are you sure we don't want to hear about Delilah's chef?"

"Yes," Delilah said. "He's a pain in the ass, and if you slept with Cal, I'm guessing he's not."

"I wouldn't rule that out. But for right now, he's not," she agreed. "I'm probably more of the ass."

"Why?" Delilah asked.

"It's just me. One of the things I've never been good at is trusting anyone. I mean, you two are about it and that's because well, you're you two. But with everyone else, it's like I'm just waiting for bad news. And I don't want to screw up Cal any more than I already have."

"Fair enough," Emma said. "He's in a rough place right now. So maybe sex was all he needed."

"But it was more than sex, wasn't it?" Delilah asked. "I saw you two at the river on Saturday."

"Yeah. I like him," she said. "So, the stakes feel higher."

Before she could say anything else, the doorbell rang and Lea and Joey joined their group, followed by Bella who was newer to Last Stand and a good friend of Delilah's. She told herself to just let her hair down and enjoy the night but she couldn't stop thinking about Cal as they all made their way over to the Last Stand Saloon.

꠸

GOOD FRIDAY. IT was hard to think about anything other than the Easter plans they'd had with Rose, TJ and Lane. It didn't really feel good in any way to him. He had spoken to Lancey—TJ's sister—on the phone this morning and she'd asked if she could take Lane for the evening. She was on leave for the weekend. He'd agreed and invited her to join them for Easter Sunday. His housekeeper was coming over early to cook a big meal for them.

He tried not to think about the little outfit hanging in the closet that Rose had purchased for Lane a month ago. She'd bought matching ties for all of the men and a dress for herself. His heart hurt as he stood there in the kitchen watching Lane play with his chicken nuggets.

The doorbell chimed. "Who dat?"

"Aunt Lancey," Cal said.

"Yay, Auntie!" Lane said, clapping his hands as he tried to wriggle out of the high chair.

"Hold your horses, buddy," Cal said, getting the tray off and then helping his nephew down. As soon as his feet were under him, he ran toward the front door, his boot heels loud on the hardwood floor. Cal followed his nephew to the door and opened it for him.

He jumped forward, hugging Lancey Maverick's legs. She looked down at Lane, tousling his hair, then glanced back at him.

Once Lancey left with their nephew, Cal and Braden had realized that the house was too quiet. They'd been staring at ESPN when Red called, asking if they wanted to join him over at the Last Stand Saloon for drinks. That had been a no-brainer, so they'd left the ranch and headed into town.

The parking lot was already starting to fill up. It was Friday night, after all. Cal found a spot and then they went inside. The jukebox was blasting 'Come Friday' by Aaron Tippin as they walked in.

"I'll get drinks while you find Red," Braden said.

Cal knew he wouldn't have to look too hard to find their

friend—he was pretty much always in the back, in the area between the dance floor and the pool tables. He had a booth and two girls were keeping him company when Cal walked up.

"Glad you could make it, dude. This is Lisa and Marjorie. They are from Whiskey River and have just spent the day on the river kayaking. Girls, this is Cal Delaney."

"Hello," they said in unison.

"Cal Delaney? The football player?" Lisa asked.

"Used to be. I'm retired," he said, grabbing a chair and pulling it up to the table.

Braden arrived with a bucket of longneck beers and smiled at the women as he sat down next to Marjorie. "Hello, ladies. I'm Braden."

"Are you a football player?" Marjorie asked.

"Nah. I make tequila."

"Red, I like your friends," Lisa quipped. "Tell me more about that. I thought you had to make it in Mexico."

"You're right. To have the tequila label, we have to grow the agave in the Tequila province. We are Mexican on our mother's side and have inherited some land down there. We run the business with our cousins," Braden said. "Cal put up the seed money to get it really going here in Last Stand."

"That's so cool," Lisa said. "I'm going to get another glass of wine. Marjorie, want one?"

Her friend nodded and Red draped his arm around Marjorie's shoulder, talking quietly to her while Braden looked at him. Seemed to them that Red wanted someone to partner up with Lisa so he could be alone with Marjorie, but he didn't need two wingmen. And Cal wasn't interested in anyone but Amelia.

He'd known that for a while. And the past few weeks had simply reinforced it. He'd driven past her place every night last week on his way home, even though it wasn't on the way, hoping for a glimpse of her.

The song changed and he heard 'Tequila Makes Her Clothes Fall Off' blaring from the jukebox. He had rolled his eyes as Lisa came back and set her wine on the table before she grabbed Braden's hand and led him to the dance floor.

"I'm going to get some fresh air," he said in the direction of Red who was twined with the woman next to him.

Cal gave the dance floor a wide berth as he made his way to the door. The saloon was busy for a holiday weekend. Normally, he'd be drinking and looking for someone who wanted nothing but fun, but tonight, he just couldn't get into the spirit. He was glad Braden had found someone to distract him even if it was just for a little while. But for himself, he needed...well, a woman he was trying not to need.

Amelia had made it very clear that she wasn't in the market for a guy on a regular basis. Neither of them was looking for that, but right now, Cal didn't feel normal and he didn't like it.

He wanted to be out there grinding up against a good-time girl who just wanted him because he had muscles and looked okay. He didn't want a woman who tied him in knots and made him miss her when she wasn't around.

He sincerely doubted a walk through town was going to

clear his head but sitting here searching the crowd for Amelia wasn't what he wanted. He put his head down, pushing through the crowd and stumbling into someone. A female someone, he thought as he reached out to steady her. Then he lifted his head and their eyes met. Amelia.

AS SOON AS she saw him, she realized how much she'd missed him. She'd been spending the evening drinking and laughing and trying to act like she was just like everyone else, even though she didn't feel it. The biggest thing about not being a real Corbyn was that she always tried to keep up appearances when she was home. Since it had only been for short weekend visits prior to this, it hadn't seemed like much of a burden.

But on the way over, Lea had been chatting to her about how jealous she was that Amelia had a family with such a long history in Last Stand. All Amelia could do was nod. She wasn't rooted here. She had no idea who Jax Williams's people were. They'd never be hers so she was rootless on that side, too. This was why she'd stayed away. It was too hard to face everyone who thought she was one thing while she knew she was something else.

"I was thinking about you," he said, under his breath. The saloon was busy tonight, as if everyone was getting their party on before family dinners and church on Sunday. She wasn't overly religious, but Memaw insisted they all attend church on Easter Sunday.

"Were you?" she asked, hoping she sounded flirty and not doubtful.

He looked good to her, with a little bit of stubble on his chin, a skintight Outlaw Tequila T-shirt and a pair of jeans that were worn in all the right places, clinging to his muscled thighs and drawing her eyes to his…um, male area.

He winked at her, letting her know that he hadn't missed her staring at his crotch. She just shrugged and tipped her head to the side. She had pretty much made herself stay busy to give him room this week. She'd heard through the grapevine that Finn had come home, having taken the week off from driving last Sunday. She knew the boys needed time together to heal. Or at least grieve together.

So, no matter how many times her car had wanted to point itself toward the Delaney ranch, she'd forced herself to stay in town, sanding old furniture that had come with her house and pretending that working on that place was more important to her than seeing Cal. She knew she should start spending more time with setting up a business but she wasn't sure she was staying. But she had a storage shed full of sanded-down furniture and every night, she lay awake in her bed aching for him and wishing he was there by her side.

"I was," he said.

"I've been thinking about you too," she said. "How have you been? I wanted to call but figured you might need some time with your family."

"You can call any time," he said. "I've been better."

"I bet. I'm sorry, Cal," she said.

He just looked away from her for a moment but not before she saw the grief and pain on his face. She couldn't imagine what he was going through and she wished there were something she could do to take that pain from him.

'Anything But Mine' by Kenny Chesney started to play. The sad, sweet song of love that wasn't meant to last made her soul ache but when Cal took her hand and drew her toward the dance floor, she didn't hesitate.

He pulled her into his arms and she rested her head on his chest as he moved her around the floor in a country waltz. She sang along under her breath but only because the words hurt. She wanted to be his. She hadn't realized it before this moment. But being Cal's was something she wished she could find her way to be.

But how could she ever trust herself? She'd been betrayed and broken for all of her adult life. She had no idea how to make anything last. Of course, this was Cal. The man who took care of everyone else, no matter the cost to himself. She knew he was no Jax Williams. But how much of her was Jax's daughter? Would she hurt him? She wouldn't be able to live with herself if she did. The price was too high, and she refused to pay it.

She'd been hurt and shut herself down. And now, as she tipped her head back and their eyes met, she wished she hadn't. But she hadn't shut Cal out. She'd never been able to do that and she now realized that she might hurt him. Again.

In that moment, she hated her mom in a way she hadn't since she'd first heard the news about her real father. She wanted to go back and be that innocent girl who'd been Cal Delaney's first serious girlfriend. She could have been his if she'd still been that girl. Not the woman who wasn't wanted. Who'd been the product of something sordid and ugly. And her whole life was a lie when she was in Last Stand.

"What are you thinking?" he asked, tucking his head down close to her, so she could hear.

But she didn't want to answer or say the truth out loud. And since lying was something she wouldn't do, she put her hands on his shoulders and went up on tiptoe, bringing her mouth to his. She felt his shock at first, but he recovered quickly, his hands sliding down to cup her butt and his mouth moving over hers. His tongue thrust into her mouth, tangling with her own.

He tasted like Lone Star Beer and dreams, she thought. But maybe that was the moonshine and lavender cocktails talking. She had never felt anything as good as being in Cal's arms.

She wanted to believe in him, believe in herself and maybe even believe in them, but her heart was too shattered for that.

She knew a better woman would walk away, would leave this sweet, sexy man for someone who would love him the way he deserved to be loved. But she couldn't.

He put one arm around her waist and lifted her off her feet as he broke the kiss. "Woman, you are killing me."

"I was trying to tempt you," she said lightly, fighting the sadness in her soul. She smiled at him. "I missed you."

"Want to get out of here?" he asked. "I know—"

She put her fingers over his lips to stop him from talking. "Yes."

Chapter Thirteen

CAL LED HER out of the Last Stand Saloon. He hoped this would be the first night of the rest of their lives. He couldn't keep doing hookups with her. Their hands were clasped together and as soon as he stepped out into the cooler air, he hesitated. He knew himself well enough to know that if he slept with Amelia again, he wasn't going to be able to keep things casual.

He liked her.

There was no denying that and more than once, he found himself waking up in the middle of the night thinking about her, wishing she was in bed next to him and that they had a more conventional relationship instead of this thing that was happening between them.

But he had no way of controlling that.

She was a goodbye girl—one who hadn't figured out enough about herself to stay. He knew he needed to acknowledge that and accept it.

"You are staring at me like you might have second thoughts," she said.

"Second and third and fourth. It always comes back to the fact that I want you in my arms, no matter the cost," he admitted.

She went up on her tiptoes, lacing her fingers together behind his neck. "There is no cost, Cal. It's just you and me together. Honestly, I've never felt anything this right with anyone else. But I'm not sure I'm staying here. My life is still back in New York."

He told himself to take that as a win but the fact that she thought this was enough was a bit of a blow. He wanted more, but didn't want to come across as needy. Too needy. Maybe it was just losing Rose and having his brothers home temporarily that was making him crave things he'd never wanted before.

But whatever it was, he needed to make up his mind about it before too much longer. But not tonight.

Tonight, he was going to take Amelia to bed and enjoy every second of it. Because she wanted him, and he wanted her.

He cupped her butt and lifted her more fully into him. She wrapped her legs around his hips, their lips met and he stopped debating with himself. It had been too long since he'd held her in his arms. That was really all he needed to know tonight.

He carried her to his truck, hearing the doors unlock as he got close, and leaning back against the passenger door for support. The skirt she wore was full and easy to get his hands under and he rubbed them up her thighs, loving the cool feel of her legs beneath his touch.

He tried to take it easy, not to clutch at her but it was hard not to. Her skin was pliant, so soft under his hands. She smelled of lavender and spring, so intoxicating and addictive. The scent aroused him as much as touching her did.

Spreading his fingers, the scent of her arousal drifted toward him. He held her, his tongue in her mouth, his erection pressing hard against the front of his jeans as he deepened the kiss.

Damn it. He didn't want to think anymore. All he needed to concentrate on was how hot he was for her. Her tongue slid along his and he sucked it deeper into his mouth. He wanted her completely naked and underneath him on a bed, but that wasn't the way they ever seemed to do it.

He ripped his mouth from hers, each exhalation of her breath brushing over his wet mouth. She bit his lower lip, licked her swollen lower one. He groaned and stopped thinking about anything but his thickening erection and how much he wanted her.

The metal of the pickup truck was cold against his back as she undulated against him. He felt her long cool fingers on his neck, stroking over his pulse, which he knew raced.

He shifted her in his arms, and seeing her erect nipples pressing against the fabric of her cotton sundress, he leaned down to suck on them through her clothing. She arched her back, thrusting her breasts toward him.

He felt the strain a little in his arms, but he'd been working out every day for most of his adult life. If he couldn't hold on to this wild cowgirl while he was making love to her, then what was the point? She moaned his name and he felt her hands in his hair, tracing the shape of his ear before moving down his neck again.

She stroked his chest and then wedged her hand between their bodies to run her fingers down the line of his zipper, over his erection. His hips jerked forward and he had to shift his hold on her. It was time.

He turned around and opened the door to the cab of his truck and lifted her up on the seat. She sat there for a minute staring down at him and he shook his head.

"Just once I'd like to make love to you in a bed."

"I'd like that, too. Think you could drive us to my place?" she asked.

"Hell yeah."

He walked around the front of the truck and got behind the wheel. He pressed the ignition start button as she scooted closer to him but he knew she needed her seat belt on. He wasn't going to be able to concentrate on anything but getting them to her place and his hard-on was making it difficult for him to drive.

"Seat belt," he said, but it came out more like a growl.

She nodded and fumbled to put it on. He drove carefully, knowing that bastard Shane Highwater would never let him live it down if he pulled him over with a woman in his truck. As soon as he pulled into the driveway of Amelia's house, he let out a sigh of relief. He put the car in park and turned it off and hopped out of the cab to go and get her. But she was already standing next to the truck and caught his hand in hers, leading him to her house.

She unlocked the door with a key that she grabbed from the top of the doorframe.

"That's not safe."

"I know. But let's not talk about it now," she said, leading him through her dark house down a hallway that led to a large master bedroom. She let go of his hand when they entered and went to turn on the bedside lamp. Then she kicked off her shoes as he stood there in the doorway.

He was taking in the room with the clean white comforter and piles of pillows when she whipped her dress up over her head and tossed it on the floor at his feet. She stood there wearing a pair of tiny panties and a lacy bra.

He fumbled to get his boots off, toeing them off one at a time and then tugged his T-shirt up over his head, wrenching his shoulder but he ignored the slight pain. He carefully undid his jeans and shoved them down his legs with his underwear.

"I do love the way you look," she said. "I haven't ever seen you totally naked before. Damn, Cal."

"Damn, yourself, honey. I'm so glad we're here and not in my truck."

She laughed and then shook her head at him. "Me too."

He hoped this night would lead to something more than lust but honestly, at this moment, with her smiling and holding her hand out to him, he didn't think he could ask for anything more.

He walked over to her, slowly because he had the feeling that if he didn't keep a tight leash on his control, he'd tumble her to the bed and it would be over too quickly.

"I always thought you were too beautiful for me," he said, the words torn from some place deep in his soul that he tried to ignore. He'd buried the hurt he felt when she'd left him but a part of him always knew it was there.

"Not at all," she said. "You used to make me feel pretty."

"You were a model, honey," he said, gently.

"To be a good model, you have to be different. I've heard all the things that are wrong with my features and my body."

"Your body?"

"My boobs are too small, my hips are a little bigger than they'd like...but that doesn't matter. I'm not modeling anymore."

"Good. Whoever said that to you was nuts. You're perfect."

"I'm glad you think so," she said.

"I do," he confirmed closing the distance between them, running his finger down the center of her torso and cupping one of her breasts. It was just right for his palm, he thought. "Perfection."

She made a soft sound and when he looked into her eyes, she blushed. "You are too good for me."

"Not at all," he said. "I'm an outlaw."

He lifted her off her feet and then carefully fell on top of her on the bed, using his hand to catch his weight. He shifted her around until she was spread out on the bed. He held her hands over her head with one hand, lowering his mouth to find hers. He kissed and nibbled.

He reached between her legs, pushing the gusset of her panties to one side. As he took his mouth from hers he shifted back on his heels to look at her. Her pubic hair was neatly trimmed and her flesh so delicate as he leaned down, parting her with his fingers. Her skin was a delicate pink and the little nub at the center swollen with need. He gently caressed her. Her hips shifted a little bit left to right. He touched her gently in a circular motion and she moaned. A sound of approval. He continued to move his finger over her before he leaned down closer.

He breathed on her skin, watching her legs fall wider apart as she lifted her hips toward him, presenting her body to him. She grabbed his head and her legs undulated next to him, one of them falling over his shoulder as he licked at her delicate flesh. He traced her core with his finger, just teasing the opening and then slowly pushed one finger up inside of her. Her hips jerked upright and he continued to nibble.

He added a second finger inside of her and thrust them deep and deeper. She was the perfect dessert on this starry night. She felt like everything to him in this moment. He was rock hard, his cock straining. He continued moving his mouth over her, until he felt her body start to tighten around his fingers. She arched her back and cried his name.

He lifted his head, pulled his fingers from her body and looked up at her. There was a flush to her body and her breath sawed in and out causing her breasts to rise and fall rapidly.

She took his erection in her hand and his hips jerked forward as she stroked him up and down. Her touch sent shudders of need through him. He'd been with a lot of women trying to forget her over the years and it was only now that he was in her arms that he realized how stupid that had been.

No other woman could make him forget Amelia.

She traced his length up and down, her fingernail scraping over his skin. She took his shaft in one hand, stroking him in her fist. Moving it up and down in a slow and sensuous movement that made his balls tighten. She skimmed her finger over the tip of his erection when she reached the top and his hips jerked forward again.

He ran his hands down her spine; she arched over him and brought her mouth down hard on his. She took one of his hands and brought it to her breast. He cupped it and then rubbed his entire body against hers, taking her hands in his and stretching them up over her head. He pushed one of his thighs between her legs and they moved to make room for his hips. He felt them come up around his waist and he shifted back until he found her opening with the tip of his erection, then slowly thrust into her.

Damn she felt so good.

She always did, he thought, but this was different. He was different this time. This time he knew he wanted her not just underneath him tonight, but in his arms forever.

He sucked her tongue deeper into his mouth as he was fully seated inside of her. He paused, letting her body adjust to his size and then she shifted, rocking back up until he was almost completely out of her before plunging back on him.

She tore her mouth from his, tipping her head back as she rode him, hard. He grabbed her hips, clutching at her buttocks, running his finger along the crease between them as he drove himself up into her and pulled her down against them. The fire of sex engulfed them both as they drove themselves harder and harder until she screamed his name and he felt her tightening around his cock. He held her hips hard against him as he continued to thrust up into her, sucking her nipple deeper into his mouth until he felt his balls tighten and he came, emptying himself as he continued to thrust into her until he was spent.

He collapsed on top of her, careful to support his own weight, tucking his head against her shoulder and letting his breath stir the hair that had come loose and hung over both of them. He pulled her into his arms and rolled to his side, scooting around on the bed until they were both under the covers and he only had one pillow under his head.

"I liked that. We're good in a bed," she said.

"We are," he said, but he didn't want to talk right now so he reached around her, turned off the light on the nightstand, then pulled her into his arms, where she curled against him. She rested her head over his heart, and he watched her until he drifted off to sleep.

Chapter Fourteen

T HE NEXT MORNING, she rolled over and found the space next to her empty. Sitting up in the bed, she stared at the pillow where Cal had rested his head and touched it, lifting it up and hugging it to her chest. It smelled faintly of his aftershave. She closed her eyes and wanted to pretend he was still with her, but the truth was, he'd been wise to leave.

She was usually the one to leave so she didn't have to wake up like this. Somehow it was different when she woke up in her own home alone. She hadn't thought this through last night. She could blame it on the moon or the moonshine or a million other things that she knew in her gut weren't the real culprits. It was Cal. And how she felt about him. She was always so careful not to allow a man—or anyone for that matter—to get too close. When she was with Cal, she felt like she was enough. That none of the secrets of her past or the dumb things she'd done when she was a teenager mattered. He made her realize she was enough. That was a gift she hadn't expected from him and one she could never hope to repay. While she didn't think that Cal had some secret he hadn't shared with her that would shake her to her core, another part of her wanted to be more cynical.

And she had been that way with all the other guys she'd had relationships with. But this was Cal. Cal, who was big and strong and always was just there for her, for his brothers, for the town. He'd slipped past her guard...distracted her with his hot body and those sultry looks he gave her.

What was she going to do?

Luckily, he left early enough that her neighbors wouldn't wake up and see his truck parked in her driveway. She wasn't flattering herself that people were watching her. They lived in a small town, after all. Gossip was the lifeblood of this place and many people would know that she'd left him when they were in high school. It wouldn't make him look good to be seen with her again.

But she missed him. She wished, not for the first time, that she'd been smarter when she'd been a teen. The choices she had made then were still rippling forward and causing repercussions she'd never even guessed at.

She heard a noise in the kitchen. Was he still here?

She got out of bed and grabbed her robe and started walking down the hall cautiously. It could be her parents or one of her sisters and honestly, the way police chief Highwater ran this town she wasn't expecting a burglar, but she shouldn't rule that out either.

She peeked around the corner and saw Cal standing there wearing nothing but his boxers, his head lowered, and his arms braced on the countertop. Next to him were two mugs and she could see the steam rising off of them.

"Cal? What is it?" she asked, going to him and wrapping

her arms around him from behind. She rested her head in the hollow between his shoulder blades and held him close. He was probably thinking of his sister and his grief. She wished she could take that away from him.

He turned in her arms, sighing as he did so. "I don't know where this is going."

"Us?" she asked, stepping back from him. Where did he want it to go? She knew he was dealing with a lot of stuff right now and she didn't want to pressure him or herself. She liked what was happening between them.

"Yeah. I know we've only hooked up twice but it feels like something more and you're the one woman who has left me, more than once, so I don't want to come off looking like a chump and expecting you to want something more than sex."

She looked at him for a long minute and then broke, letting her gaze fall to the floor. What did she expect? What did she want? She hadn't thought about the impact of her actions on Cal. She had left him twice. Once of course she'd been young, but she'd cared about him. She should have talked to him that night. And then of course there was the evening on his porch swing, right after his sister's death. She'd just walked away.

"I don't know. I'm not going to lie to you ever, Cal, but honestly, I don't know what's next. I like you. I always have. But there is also this part of me that is always holding back, that's afraid to let myself really care for you in case…"

"In case what? I'm not your folks. Hell, I'm not even the guy who sired you and walked away. It's me, Cal Delaney, who you've known your entire life. The guy who used to always pick you for my team at recess because I liked your smile. I need you to be all in on this. Because I can pretend that I'm cool with whatever you say when I'm not," he said. "Damn me. My timing sucks because I know this looks like me being needy because of everything that happened with Rose—"

"It doesn't. You're not that kind of guy, Cal. I've known that even when I wasn't sure of anything else. You're solid. You always know what you're going to do, and you don't hesitate."

"How is that a bad thing?" he asked.

"I don't know. I just know that I'm not sure of myself and if I hurt you, I'd never be able to live with myself. And it's not just you I'd hurt but little Lane too. I don't want to do that."

But really, did she need him to say it out loud to confirm what she already knew? She was one of those people who tried to always be honest even when the cost was high. She felt the pain in her stomach and in her heart as she stood in front of him. She'd hurt him in a way that she'd never wanted to. And now the one man she'd let slip past her guard was asking her not to do it again. Not to hurt him again and she couldn't promise she wouldn't. She couldn't promise that she wouldn't feel scared and bolt as she had before.

Both continued to stare at each other and she realized his silence was the answer she didn't want to hear.

CAL DIDN'T KNOW how to answer her. He wanted to be honest, but he could already see the hurt on her face. He just didn't want to be one more person in her life who did that to her. In the back of his mind, he heard his dad's voice telling him he was a pussy when it came to women. Gotta love the old man and his "blunt" talk. But there was some truth to it. He loved her.

Damn.

He did love her.

Well hell, he'd probably loved her since she left him back in high school. But he'd been able to ignore it because life had a lot to offer him when he'd been a star football player, recruited to play college ball and then moving on to the pros. He'd been a top ten draft pick and an all-star but none of that mattered.

Same as it didn't really matter who Amelia's daddy was or what she thought about any of that. He still loved her and nothing was going to change that. He just had to figure out exactly how much he could take.

Grief for Rose and guilt about TJ weighed heavy on him. He could let himself fall into that as a distraction from the pain of knowing he loved her and she wasn't ready to even commit to more than sleeping together occasionally.

He should just walk away.

But it was Amelia.

"You can say it," she said. "We both know it. Coming home for Mom didn't change who I was."

"I never said it did." Her pain had formed her into the woman she was today. She was strong and sexy and sweet. But she couldn't trust. Not really. Could he gamble his heart and his future on her?

He wanted to think that it wouldn't be a gamble. Braden had always said he had the devil's own luck with women; except with Amelia, he felt like he was the one drowning in temptation.

"I wish it had. I wish hearing the explanation of why she did what she did made it all okay, but I still can't square that with something inside of me. I feel broken and not good enough," she said, wrapping her arms around her waist and he wanted to go to her, wrap her in his arms and reassure her she was enough. More than enough.

But he wasn't the man she needed to hear that from. And until she made her peace with her past and with Jax Williams, she was never going to be able to move forward. This wasn't his battle to fight. Not one he could go in and fight for her. He knew that. He wished it was different but wishing had never changed anything.

"I'm sorry for the shit hand you got dealt and that you had to deal with all of it when you weren't old enough to really get it," he said at last. He finally realized why Rose had kept trying with TJ. She had told Cal how much she loved her boyfriend and he had dismissed it because until this moment, he'd never loved anyone that much.

But now he did.

And it sucked. He couldn't fix her or fix things for her. He couldn't make her stay much the same way Rose hadn't been able to keep TJ by her side. Cal knew he was going to have to let her go. Walk away from her this time and if it was right…if it was meant to be, she'd come back to him.

"I'm sorry I didn't realize the impact of my actions. I was so selfish and scared that it never occurred to me that what I was doing would have a lasting effect on you," she said.

He nodded. "It's okay. I haven't had it that bad. My life is good and I think it would be even better with you, honey, if you would just take a chance."

She nodded, but it was too quick to be sincere and he knew that deep in his soul. She nibbled on her lower lip and a part of him thought he should just take her back to bed and then leave while she was showering or sleeping or something like that. But if he slept with her again, he'd never recover. If he ended this now, in her kitchen with the smell of spring flowers and coffee in the air, he might be able to move on.

Even as he told himself that, he knew it was a lie. But he shook that off. If he was leaving her—and he was definitely going to do that—he needed to believe that it wasn't forever.

"It's not the past that I'm concerned about. We were kids."

"We were. I don't know what you want from me. I could lie and say sure I want something more but, in the end, I don't know what's going to happen between us," she said. "And then it would still hurt. But this way we can just enjoy being with each other—"

"I can't. I want more," he admitted.

"Okay. That's it then. There is no middle ground—"

"What kind of middle ground? I love you, Amelia. I'm not going to pretend that I don't care for you or that I think I could care about you. I'm not someone who runs around telling women he loves them all the time. But you are different. I guess I've always known that. But taking whatever you can give me? Making do with less than what I know what we could have if you'd just let go of your past? I can't do that."

"I didn't ask you to," she said.

"Good, because I won't. You know my family history. You know how cursed we are at love, but we still keep trying, each new generation hoping they'll be the ones to break the curse... But instead, we fall again and again for someone who is destined to break them."

SHE TURNED AWAY from him and walked over to the window that looked out over her backyard. The yard was overgrown and needed a lot of work. That had been part of the appeal when she'd come back to Last Stand. A chance to be outside, something she'd never had a chance to do when she was in New York. To take the time she needed to fix the areas of life that needed fixing.

But as soon as she'd seen Cal, everything had gotten messed up in her head. She'd lost herself in him. He was the one guy she'd known before her life had gotten screwed up and she had always thought he was different. But he wasn't a man who was good at waiting around and she couldn't ask him to.

She needed to sort herself out. She had been using him because he made her feel good. And she suspected he had been using her too. Using her to avoid thinking too much about Rose and his nephew. His life had majorly changed and they had jumped into sleeping together because…well for herself, she'd needed to comfort him and be with him.

She didn't know why he'd done it. He said he loved her but she knew that it took longer than a few weeks to fall in love. Didn't it? She'd never been in love with a guy or had one fall for her.

Of course, her dad had said he'd fallen for her mom in a few hours. But she wasn't sure she could trust her feelings.

"I think you need time too," she said at last. "You are dealing with a big change in your family—"

"I know what I'm dealing with. And I've got this. I always have."

He definitely always had. Cal had been the one the boys and Rose had turned to even when they were kids. He'd always taken care of everyone. She wished she were different, so she could be the one who took care of him. She thought that she was doing that with sex, but he needed more from her than that. She knew it now. Maybe she had always known it but hadn't wanted to admit it.

"You're right. But you are definitely using this as a distraction to keep you from dealing with—"

"Don't. Don't try to tell me that I'm compartmentalizing my life. I know that I am. I've been doing it since my high school girlfriend slept with me and then ghosted. Hell, I think I've been doing it since my mom died. It's how I survive, and it works."

"I wasn't asking you to change," she said quietly.

"I know you weren't. I'm going to get out of here. I'll see you around," he said, walking out of the kitchen and down the hall to the bedroom. She heard him moving around and stood there like she was rooted to the spot. This hurt worse than just about anything she'd ever experienced because she knew that he wouldn't come back to her. And she wasn't sure she would be able to change enough to be the woman he needed her to be.

She wanted to cry but wouldn't let herself do it until he came out of her bedroom all dressed, his boot heels ringing in her empty house and walked out the door. She stood there by the back door, refusing to look out and watch him leave, but she heard the hemi motor in his truck as he roared out of her driveway and down her street. Only then did she stumble to the kitchen table and collapse into the chair. She put her head on her arms and cried.

She didn't try to pretend that it wasn't heartbreak making her cry. She loved Cal. She knew that. But what he wanted from her was more than she was ever going to be able to give. Letting him leave her was the only option that had made any sense but it hurt far worse than she had expected.

She wasn't someone who gave up easily. She'd gone after a career as a high-end model and had been very successful at it, but in relationships, it was different. In her career, she had never felt like she had anything to lose, but in relationships she always—always found herself like this.

Alone.

Damn, she was starting to feel sorry for herself.

Her phone rang. Not her cell phone but the landline that her parents had insisted she have installed when she moved back home. She ignored it at first but then realized it could be about her mom.

She stood up so quickly the chair fell over as she ran to grab the handset of the phone from the wall.

"Hello."

"It's Dad. I'm taking your mom to the hospital. She's not responsive. Call your sisters and meet me there," he said.

"Okay, Dad. We'll be right there. Love you."

"Love you too, honey."

He hung up and she called her sisters and then went to pick them up. The entire time she was trying to ignore the one fact that she couldn't anymore. She thought she'd been protecting herself by leaving Last Stand. By letting Cal go and her parents go. But the truth was, love was there in her heart and in her soul the entire time. And no matter how strong she'd believed she was, she knew that it was that love that added the steel to her backbone and the strength to her life.

As she watched her father standing in the waiting area, anxious to hear about her mom, she recognized the look in his eyes. Realized that the pain and the fear was the same thing she'd seen in Cal's eyes that morning. And she knew she had to figure out a way to love him and get him back into her life.

Chapter Fifteen

CAL WASN'T IN any mood to talk to his brothers and as soon as he got home, he went into his office and closed the door. But that didn't deter either of them.

Finn didn't even bother knocking. He just came in and plopped down on the leather sofa and stretched his legs out in front of him. "Didn't expect to see you today. I heard you left the saloon last night with Amelia."

"Yeah, so what of it?" Cal said. He knew he sounded belligerent but the last thing he wanted was talk about her.

"Dude, you're not doing it right if you are pissed off when you leave your woman," Finn said.

"I'm doing it just fine," he said.

"I wasn't critiquing you, just saying that…do you think she's the right woman for you?" Finn asked. "I remember when she left—just because it was right before things started taking off for me and you were messed up for a while."

"Yeah, thanks for reminding me," he said. "I know I seem like some sort of dumb asshole for hooking up with her, Finn. You don't have to point it out."

"I don't think that at all," he said. "I know you. You aren't someone who just sleeps around as much as you might want to come off that way."

He didn't want to discuss this. He thought of the women he'd been in relationships with, now that Finn had brought them up. He'd had some really good women care for him and tell him that they loved him over the years, but he'd always been the one who didn't want to commit. Now it seemed that was all down to Amelia. His feelings for her had been buried deep inside, just lying dormant and waiting until she came back.

"I like being a loner; you know that, right? I'm not one of those guys who has to be in a relationship to feel like I'm successful," he said.

"I know. But she's different and she always has been," Finn said. "I don't know about Braden but you and me, we've always been good about keeping moving so nothing can tie us down. But Amelia, she knew you before you realized that running was the only thing that could keep you safe."

When had Finn gotten so smart about women? "That's really wise."

"Thanks. I can't take credit for it. Rose said it to me the last time I was home. She was always way older than her years."

"She was. And the smartest of all of us. Don't let Braden know I said that."

"Too late," Braden said, coming into the room. "I heard you. But I agree. I miss her."

"I do too," Cal admitted.

"We're not doing this," Finn said. "I don't want to talk

about her being gone."

"Why not?" Braden said. "Ignoring your feelings isn't going to make them go away."

Cal knew that his brother was talking to Finn, but the truth was that the words applied to his relationship with Amelia as well. But he didn't have another option. He needed to get out of Last Stand.

"Bray, I think I'm going to go to Mexico for a few weeks. Javier has some new agave tanks and I haven't been down there in a few months. Can you handle things without me?"

"Yeah, I always can but are you sure you want to leave?" Braden asked. "Looked like things were heating up between you and Amelia last night."

He was definitely sure he wanted to leave. "Looks can be deceiving. How'd it go with you and the lady from Whiskey River?"

"Good. She was what I needed last night. But that's not the same thing as you and Ame—"

"I don't want to talk about this," Cal said. "I need to get out of town and get my perspective back."

"Then go. Finn leaves all the time too," Braden said. "I'm used to holding down the fort. I guess this time, it will be me and Lane. But that's fine too. I've never seen whatever it is that pulls y'all out of here."

Finn turned to look at Braden then glanced back at him. "I can't speak for Cal, but it isn't something out there. It's always been something or someone here."

Braden came further into the room and sat on the arm of the sofa, his brow crinkled as he looked down at Finn. "Who are you running from?"

"Dad at first. Then the mess with Rose. I didn't want to be Dad and say all the wrong things and call it tough love...you know?"

"I do know," Braden said. "What about you, Cal?"

"Same. But also out there, I'm just Cal. I'm not one of those Delaneys, little better than outlaws. Generations of law breaking, drinking and curses don't follow me when I'm not in Last Stand. There's a certain freedom to it."

"Then go," Braden said. "I like being a Delaney. Even one of those Delaneys—it grounds me. Gives me something to lean on when I'm feeling like the nerdy, skinny kid who used to get bullied for his lunch money."

"We took care of that bully for you," Finn said.

"I know. But y'all are gone now. I have to take of them for myself and every time I start feeling cowardly, I remember how badass our ancestors were and make myself do it."

Cal got up and went over to Braden, squeezing his shoulder. "I do the same thing. I think we all feel like that."

"Yeah?" Braden asked, looking over at him from behind his horn-rimmed glasses.

He nodded at his brother and then looked around the room. Braden was right. He couldn't keep running away whenever things got tough. He'd check out the business in Mexico, but only for a few days. And then he'd come home. And if he saw Amelia, he'd remind himself they had a good run and he wanted more...no matter how hard that might be to believe. This was his town and it was time to change the way that everyone thought of the Delaneys, starting with himself and his brothers.

AMELIA AND HER sisters took turns sitting next to their mom and watching over her. They finally had a diagnosis, which meant they could start treating it—West Nile virus. They were all incredibly worried but had spoken to the doctor who had treated several patients who had survived. The biggest thing was to get it under control. Her mom was sleeping with a breathing tube and had an IV drip with medication in it. In all her life, Amelia had never seen her mom look so vulnerable.

She'd always been so tough and projected herself as if she were taller than her five feet, three inches. She'd been indomitable, so seeing her like this scared Amelia and made her very angry with herself that she'd waited so long to come back home and forgive her mom.

She thought about all that Cal had revealed this morning and how she'd always felt like she had the moral high ground when she'd left, but was she really any different than her parents, who'd kept that big secret? Or Jax Williams, who'd had sex with her mom and never looked back?

She hadn't set out to hurt Cal but she'd done it all the same. She'd taken from him what she needed and walked away.

She always thought of herself as a nice person but since she'd come back she'd had to face the fact that she was a user. True, she'd never intended to hurt him, but she had all the same.

She felt tears burning her eyes and wiped them away. "Are you okay?"

She glanced over to see Emma standing there with two Bluebonnet Café takeaway cups. Her sister's long reddish-brown hair hung around her shoulders as she watched her.

"No," she said. "I have just realized how selfish I've been my entire adult life."

"I think you're being a little melodramatic," Emma said handing her a cup and sitting down next to her. "I don't want to be unkind, but you have bags under your eyes, so I know you're overtired. Also, you didn't say what happened with Cal...and I'm guessing something did because he didn't come with you to the hospital."

She took a sip of the chai tea her sister had brought and then glanced at her mom. "Ems, I don't know what's wrong with me. Cal wanted to...like have a relationship and I couldn't just say, sure. I like him—heck, I think I love him, but the thought of committing to him and then finding out he had some secret...well I just couldn't do it. And I couldn't lie to him so that he'd think I was okay with it until we were together enough for me to believe it."

Emma reached over and took her hand in hers. Squeezing it. "That's nothing to do with you. I feel that way too about relationships."

Of course, her sister did. Emma had always preferred reading to interacting with people. "Thanks. But there's more."

"Like what?"

"I'm not a very nice person," she admitted.

"Cal said that to you?" Emma asked, turning in her chair. "That had to be the grief talking. He has been through a lot lately."

"Yes, he has. But he didn't say it. In fact, he was sort of like, I'd have done the same thing, but you know he wouldn't have."

"What did you do?" Emma asked.

She leaned in closer to her sister. "The night before I left for New York, Cal and I slept together. I just wanted my first time to be with someone I genuinely liked and...I never told him I was leaving, mainly because we were in high school and it was weird after and he dropped me off. I never thought of how that impacted him."

Her voice shook a little as she fought to control her emotions and then realized she was crying. Why was she crying? She'd apologized but really, could words make up for that? And it wouldn't matter so much if she didn't love him. And she did love him. Way more than she'd ever expected to.

"Oh, Ams, I'm so sorry that happened that way. I'm sure that he doesn't blame you," Emma said, rubbing her back.

"He doesn't. That makes it even worse, like I know I was horrible to him but he's still so decent and he loves me. But I can't even commit to just being with him other than casually. Makes me feel like an asshole...I am an—"

"You're not. Don't call yourself names. If you love him then why can't you take a chance on him?" Emma asked. "Is it that you don't believe you deserve love?"

She shifted away from her sister back into her chair and

wiped her eyes. Was that it? "I think it might be. I mean for as long as I can remember, I have tried to keep everyone at arm's length but that was never an option with Cal. I mean he's always been my touchstone sort of."

"Then he's always been there…it's never been casual to you. Have you thought of that?"

"I hadn't," she admitted but saying it out loud had changed things in her mind. She could see now that it wasn't Cal she was afraid of, but herself. He would never let her down, he never had. Plus, Cal was pretty much a tell-it-as-it-is kind of guy so he'd never hide anything from her.

It had been her own fear of not wanting to be hurt the way she had been again. "I hope it's not too late to try to win him back."

"Of course, there's enough time," Mom said from the bed, her voice weak. "Love always finds a way."

"Mom!"

They both rushed to her side talking at the same time and hugging her. Amelia texted her dad and Delilah so they could get back from the café where they were taking a break to eat breakfast.

"You scared us," Amelia said.

"I'm sorry," Mom said.

Her dad rushed in and moved straight to their mom's side, hugging her gently. They all saw the tears in his eyes as he looked down at her. "I thought I'd lost you."

"Never," she said. "You can tell me what's going on. Amelia, go sort things out with Cal."

"Yes, ma'am."

"What's going on?" Delilah asked.

"I'll catch you up," Emma said as Amelia grabbed her bag and headed out of the hospital.

Sure, it was all well and good to think she could fix things with Cal but how was she going to convince him that she'd changed…well actually, she hadn't changed. She'd just finally stopped hiding from the truth. That loving him was the one thing that had always been deep inside of her.

DECIDING SHE WANTED to change things with Cal and actually changing them were two very different things. She had gone home on Sunday afternoon and slept for a few hours and decided Monday would be soon enough to go and talk to him. But when she went to the Outlaw Tequila offices on Monday Braden told her that Cal had gone to Mexico for a few weeks.

Then she got a call from one of her old brands asking her to come and shoot a campaign in New York, which she did, so it was the middle of June before she was back in Last Stand. Her mom was doing a lot better and was responding well to treatment. She had to use a cane for walking, but her mind was clearer, which her doctor said was the first step to recovery.

Amelia had made up her mind to go out to the Delaney ranch and wait for Cal but her memaw had called with a royal summons demanding that she come for dinner. So after she finished with her last class of the day, instead of going to see Cal, she was on her way to Memaw's house.

Amelia freely admitted she was a bit worried about what her grandmother wanted since the last time she'd received one of these summonses, it had been after she'd updated her will and wanted to make sure she and her sisters were told which of her memaw's stuffed dogs they were going to receive when she passed.

She pulled into the driveway and noticed that Cal's truck was parked there. She swallowed hard and then got out of her car and walked around back, stopping when she saw Cal sitting on the bed swing in the backyard. All of the things she wanted to say to him slipped from her mind.

He looked so good just sitting there and it was all she could do not to run over and throw herself into his arms. She'd missed him so much.

"I am so glad to see you," she said.

"Me too," he said.

They both stared at each other, the heat of the Texas June evening building around them, and she leaned in closer and finally just thought, screw it. There was no way she was going to let him leave again without telling him how she felt.

"I've been—"

"I wanted to—"

He shook his head and stood up, walked over to her. "Ladies first."

"Um, well, as soon as you left that morning, I felt this gaping hole inside of me and I couldn't figure out what I was going to do about it because I realized I'd been lying to myself for a while now about you. That I ever thought we were just casual was ridiculous. I love you, Cal."

"You do?"

"I have loved you for a while…after that time on the porch. I went out there to comfort you but as I left, I knew you meant something to me. I was just so afraid to admit it. Afraid that I wouldn't be able to make it work."

He didn't say anything, just kept watching her. "You know I love you. I told you that the morning I left and that hasn't changed."

"Really?"

"Yeah. I think I've loved you forever."

Her heart felt so full and she couldn't keep herself from launching herself toward him and he caught her. She wrapped her arms around his shoulders and her legs around his hips. She looked down into his face and saw all the love she'd always been afraid to admit that she wanted. It was there on his face and in his heart.

She kissed him. Deeply, trying to show him how much he meant to her. She held him as tightly as she could.

He broke the kiss and turned to walk back to the bed swing, sitting down with her on it, holding her close. "Are you sure?"

"Yes, I am," she said. But she knew it would take time for them both to believe it. And that was okay. The important thing was that they were together. Time would prove to them that their love was as strong as they believed it was.

"Me too. I want to take this slow and make sure, for both of our sakes. But I'm never letting you go again," he said.

"I'm not letting you go either," she vowed.

Just then they heard a sigh from the garden shed and glanced over to see Memaw and her friend Clara Perkins watching them. Clara was notorious in town for her matchmaking and seeing her and Memaw together didn't really surprise Amelia.

"Took y'all long enough. Thought I was going to have to hogtie you both to get you to stop being so stubborn," Priscilla said.

"Memaw!"

"Sorry, honey, but I have to agree with Priscilla. You two were taking the Lord's own sweet time to admit what the rest of us could already see."

Cal shook his head. "I guess it's official then. We're a couple. You okay with that?"

"Better than okay!"

Epilogue

C AL AND LANE came with her to New York to pack up her apartment on the Upper East Side. Having them by her side made her realize that her career success had been a pale substitute for the kind of love she'd always craved.

She and Cal were working on fixing up her place in Last Stand but she'd moved out to the Delaney ranch with him. Lane's custody was being contested by Lancey, who had gotten out earlier from the Marines and wanted to help raise him.

Even so Amelia and Lane had formed a bond that would stay strong. She was determined to make it that way. She'd realized that blood didn't determine how much a parent loved a child...the parent did.

That realization had been a long time coming and she knew that most of the reason for that was on her shoulders. She'd been afraid to believe she could really be a Corbyn when all the time she'd always been one.

Cal came up behind her and Lane slipped his hand into hers.

"Ready to go home?"

"Definitely," she said. No more running for her. Now she knew where her home was. It was anywhere she was with Cal.

The End

If you enjoyed this book, please leave a review at your favorite online retailer!

Even if it's just a sentence or two it makes all the difference.

Thanks for reading *Her Texas Ex* by Katherine Garbera!

Discover your next romance at TulePublishing.com.

TULE
PUBLISHING

Love the town of Last Stand, Texas? Stay awhile. Where the women are feisty, the men are sexy and the romance is hotter than ever.

Last Stand, Texas

Heart of the Texas Doctor by Eve Gaddy

Her Texas Ex by Katherine Garbera

The Lone Star Lawman by Justine Davis

A Son for the Texas Cowboy by Sinclair Jayne

The Perfect Catch by Joanne Rock

Available now at your favorite online retailer!

Love the town of Whiskey River, Texas? Stay awhile. Where the women are feisty, the men are sexy and the romance is hotter than ever.

The Brothers of Whiskey River Series

Book 1: **Texas Heirs** by Eve Gaddy and Katherine Garbera

Book 2: **Texas Cowboy** by Eve Gaddy

Book 3: **Texas Tycoon** by Katherine Garbera

Book 4: **Texas Rebel** by Eve Gaddy

Book 5: **Texas Lover** by Katherine Garbera

Book 6: **Texas Bachelor** by Eve Gaddy and Katherine Garbera

Available now at your favorite online retailer!

About the Author

USA Today bestselling author **Katherine Garbera** is a two-time Maggie winner who has written more than 60 books. A Florida native who grew up to travel the globe, Katherine now makes her home in the Midlands of the UK with her husband, two children and a very spoiled miniature dachshund.

Thank you for reading

Her Texas Ex

If you enjoyed this book, you can find more from all our great authors at TulePublishing.com, or from your favorite online retailer.

TULE
PUBLISHING

Made in the USA
Monee, IL
31 January 2020

21139288R00116